A WOMAN FOR ALL REASONS

BY

PAUL CHANDLER

AND

NICK GOODMAN

A WOMAN FOR ALL REASONS

Also by Paul Chandler, available at www.lulu.com/spotlight/shyyeti

Shy Yeti's Grrr-eatest Hits (2018)
The Shy Yeti Sketch Book (2018)
Pieces Of Shy Yeti (2019)

Also available on Amazon and in your ears via:
The Shy Life Podcast: https://shyyeti.libsyn.com/

Also by Nick Goodman, available at
www.lulu.com/spotlight/nickaly

The Noughties Video Scripts
The Nineties Video Scripts – Volumes One and Two
Run Faster Than the World: Script and Post-Script
Cradle Snatcher, Decimated!, The Dominoes, Sanctum, Sunset Whaddon

Magnet Memories – The Story of a Secret Series, 1977-1987
by Nick Goodman and Jo Bunsell (Hidden Tiger)

Life After Magnet Memories – The Return of the Secret Series, 1988-94
by Nick Goodman, Jo Bunsell and Paul Chandler (Hidden Tiger)

BRIEF PREMISE

Matt is trying to help his best friend, Bob, through a writer's block – involving him in a local mystery involving an inhabitant who appears to be over-150 years old.

They begin to piece together a number of clues by speaking to a rather eccentric librarian named Emily and her assistant, Kirsten who are colleagues of Matt's from the upstairs Reference section of the library.

Meanwhile, Bob's wife – Debs – isn't coping so well with her husband gallivanting around the town at all hours of the night and she has confided her concerns to her trusty Aunt Alice…

Much to Deb's dismay Alice takes a far deeper interest in the whole matter than she had ever imagined – tracing Bob and Matt's footsteps to try and discover what exactly they have been up to!

Meanwhile, elsewhere – things are really beginning to get out of hand…

Will the clues come together to provide an answer?

Will Bob's marriage survive their adventure?

What does a strange man named CB know about the whole matter?

So much about the past remains in the shadows – is this one mystery which simply refuses to be solved?

WRITING CREDITS:

A WOMAN FOR ALL REASONS was written between the 2nd July 2016 and the 24th December 2019

Additional re-writes, formatting of the text and the hunting out of typos and small re-writes were made by Paul Chandler between July and August 2020 and later by Martin AW Holmes during Spring 2022.

The following episodes were written by Paul Chandler: 1, 3, 5, 7, 9

The following episodes were written by Nick Goodman: 2, 4, 6, 8, 10, End-game (11)

MANY THANKS TO MARTIN HOLMES FOR ALL HIS HELP…

MAIN CHARACTERS:

Lady Constance L.P. Walsh –   The cause of all the mystery
Matthew ("Matt") Spencer –   An assistant librarian
Bob Tully –   A truck driver / delivery man
Debra Tully (Debs) –   Bob's wife
Auntie Alice (Alice Harrison) –   Deb's aunt Emily
Emily Bradnock –   Senior library clerk
Kirsten –   Library clerk
CB (Jake Treherne) –   An eccentric shack dweller
Graham –   Employee at "The Luminary Tavern"

Police Constable Carr –   Policeman
Superintendent Tavistock –   Policeman
Darcy –   Drinker at "the Luminary Tavern"
Edmund –   A rich collector of comic books
Hercules –   Personal assistant to "man"
Edmund's Mother –   Long suffering mother
"Man" –   Un-named husband of tv-watching "woman"

"Woman" –   Un-named wife of tv-watching "man"

Georgio –   Housekeeper of "man" and "woman"

Miss Jameson –   An enthusiastic schoolteacher
Chloe –   A four-year-old girl
The Marquis of Hamilton –   A gentleman with a dark past
Lewis –   Kirsten's son
Anonymous Mother –   Appreciative of CB's performance!?
Tim –   DJ on the local Radio Station
Pam –   Tim's Producer at the Radio Station

CHAPTERS

A WOMAN FOR ALL REASONS

EPISODE ONE: OUT OF A RUT...

BY PAUL CHANDLER

(Matt and Bob are two middle aged men who have known each other for many years. Their friendship emerged from a shared love of 'Cult TV' and films – they are also keen writers, although of late Bob appears less inspired and Matt is concerned by how it is affecting him. On the night that this scene takes place they have both gone to the pub to put the world to rights and predictably the subject of their writing comes up.)

SCENE 1: INT. THE UNRULY PHEASANT PUB. NIGHT.

MATT:

Listen, I've had this great idea. You don't have to say yes – well, not straight away – but I do want you to consider it. Okay?

BOB:

Hmm. I'm not sure that I like the sound of this.

MATT:

Bear with me – it'll be fun. I promise.

BOB:

Yeah, well, alright. But before you break whatever it is that you're going to tell me; do you want another drink?

MATT:

In a minute, the booze can wait – you've got to hear this. Sorry, I don't mean to be rude, mate – but I do want to tell you my idea first. I've been running my sales pitch through my head for nearly a week now and if I'm not careful I'm not going to do it justice and just sound stupid.

6

BOB:

Aw, come on now – I'm sure you know what you're talking about!
Waiting is fine by me. I've still got some of my pint – you're the one
sitting with an empty glass; but maybe you need a clear head for this
speech of yours!

MATT: *(somewhat impatiently)*

I'd not even noticed I was empty; no matter – so now, may I speak?

BOB: *(with a grin)*

Go ahead. I'm listening! I'm not stopping you – go on – go on...

MATT: *(matter-of-fact)*

Well, you see – it's simple; I think we should write something together.

BOB: *(surprised)*

Really?

What brought this on?

You short of ideas?

MATT:

Don't be mean. No, I'm not short of ideas – that's not the point. I just
thought it would be nice to write something together – we've done it
before; just not for ages – decades even.

BOB: *(grumpily)*

I'm not a charity case, you know. I know what you're up to.

MATT: *(reasoning)*

Nobody said you WERE a charity case; but I know you've been wanting

7

to write something; I just thought that working together might help.

BOB: *(sounding slightly unsure)*

Well, okay then; sure, I'd love to; I'm certainly lacking in inspiration!

MATT:

Yes, I know – and it's been a while... Well, anyway – I have a subject that we can both collaborate on and maybe see where the idea goes.

BOB:

I do hope that this isn't one of your usual daft ideas – you know, with space aliens, talking aspidistra and the like.

MATT:

That never happened. I never wrote that script; well, not yet.

BOB:

Hmm, I find that hard to believe. Why not? It sounds fun!

MATT:

Oh, you know – I just hadn't got round to it yet – give me time. Anyway, that's not the sort of thing I was thinking about. Can I tell you more?

BOB:

Yes! Okay. Go on, then. But this time I AM going to visit the bar first. We both have empty glasses now; I think this is going to be a long night!

MATT:

Marvellous! But please, let me go.

BOB:

Really? But it's MY round.

MATT:

Ah well – not any more. I want to celebrate our new writing venture.

BOB:

Oh, go on then... Who am I to get in the way of the last of the big spenders!

MATT:

Ha! Same again?

BOB:

I think I'll have a double.

MATT:

A double lager?

BOB:

Yeah, why not. We're meant to be celebrating, right?

MATT:

Absolutely! Okay, then. Whatever the lady wants. Don't go away.

(Matt heads to the bar – Bob just shakes his head with a smile; however, he does seem brighter and more engaged than he did a few moments ago)

SCENE 2: INT. BOB'S HOUSE – SOME TIME LATER

(It is almost midnight, but Bob's wife – Debs is waiting up, half-asleep in front of one of her favourite blood-thirsty detective series. Attempting to revive herself as she hears him removing his coat and shoes in the hall, she quickly rubs her eyes and tries to look more awake – presenting Bob with a welcoming smile as he shuffles clumsily into the lounge.)

DEBS: *(surprised)*

On your own?

BOB:

Yeah, Matt's flagging. He says hi though. How are you doing, honey? I hope you've had a good night. Did you miss me?

DEBS:

I'm fine. Keeping entertained! Felicity Muggeridge just got impaled!

BOB:

Bad luck, Felicity... Oh... WHO is Felicity Muggeridge, by the way?

DEBS: *(casually, she chuckles)*

She's the Mayor's wife, love – pay attention.

BOB: *(playing catch-up)*

Not in real life, right? On one of your shows.

DEBS: *(grinning)*

On one of my shows, yes.

BOB:

What's it called again? THE BLOOD AND GUTS SHOW?

DEBS: *(straight-faced)*

Almost! Inspector Lambert Investigates.

BOB: *(playfully)*

Oh... I much prefer The Blood and Guts Show – they should re-title it!

DEBS: *(nonplussed)*

Yeah... Right.

BOB: *(teasing)*

You really must tell me more, love; only wait until I'm asleep.

DEBS: *(with mock disgust, then back to normal)*

Charming! You want a cocoa or something?

BOB:

It's okay. I'll make it. Do you want one?

DEBS:

Oh, please. So, what's up – you look a bit thoughtful about something.

BOB:

It's Matt – he's had an idea and I've said yes and now I'm not sure.

DEBS:

Oh dear. I knew I should have gone with you! It's not another sci-fi convention in some dreary marquee in Reading, is it?

11

BOB:

No – And I'll have you know that it wasn't half as dreary as you make it out to be. Everybody was really friendly, and I bought a very nice t-shirt.

DEBS:

Alright, alright – so what's he got you mixed up with this time?

BOB:

He's suggested that we do a writing project together.

DEBS: *(relieved/pleased/curious)*

So? What's wrong with that – you've been wanting to write something for ages now – it'll be good for you two to have a shared project again.

BOB:

Sure, yes. I agree. He wants us to do some research in the local library – he's got some leads about something that happened years ago.

DEBS: *(mockingly, yet affectionately so)*

Not the time his granny's cat got stuck in the tree and it made the front page – when was that? 1967? Earlier?

BOB:

1968! No, I don't think it's that; it sounds mysterious! We're going to meet at the weekend when you're at your sister's and talk over it more then. I'm not sure where it'll lead us – but I'll admit I'm curious.

DEBS:

I'd declare it as a case for Inspector Lambert if only he wasn't fictional!

BOB:

Don't be cruel. Have you been at the sherry again? *(Debs pulls a face)* No… Don't even bother to answer that. I wouldn't blame you if you had, considering the tosh that you've been watching all night.

DEBS:

Aw! Come on, I'm only teasing. I'm pleased for you! Pleased for Matt too. That cat stuck up the tree will finally have his metaphorical day in the sun! Matt's clearly identified the dog who chased it up there and wants you to turn the whole story into some kind of sensationalist pot-boiler. Shame they're all dead now – maybe you'll be able to speak to one of the doggy relatives and get some first-hand barking that you can quote at the end.

BOB: *(pretending to take offence)*

I'm not listening. You're just being silly. Even more than usual.

DEBS: *(pursuing her point, flippantly)*

No, Bob; I'm serious! Matt might be due some reparations connected to his granny's estate. It might be worth him looking into.

BOB:

You can be horribly sarcastic at times, you know – I'm just glad Matt isn't here to hear you say these things. I'm going to ignore you now and make the cocoa. It's that poor dead cat that I feel sorry for. Have you no respect?

DEBS:

I know. I know. I'm a terrible person, I really am – thank goodness I have you to set me back on the straight and narrow. I think cocoa is probably a good idea. Might sober me up too. I'll have a biscuit too whilst you're out there, love. *(there is no reply, she continues – still clearly finishing herself very amusing)* Hey?! Bob. Did you hear me!? I said I'd like a biscuit – why not just bring in the whole barrel.

(But Bob is in the kitchen and pretends not to hear – he shakes his head as he switches on the kettle – he isn't upset for he is used to his wife's daft sense of humour. In fact, it is one of the things that bonds them)

SCENE 3: INT. MATT'S HOUSE – NEXT EVENING

(Matt is just back from work, distractedly he is stroking the head of his cat, a ginger tom called Tolstoy – when the phone starts to ring... He answers it – the number comes up as Bob's home phone number)

MATT:

Bob? What's up? I thought you were working late, tonight? If I'd have known, we could have arranged to meet up to discuss my idea!

DEBS:

Sorry, Matt… He is working late... It's me... Debs...

MATT: *(surprised but pleased)*

Oh! Hey! Hello, dear lady... How can I help?

DEBS:

What are you up to?

MATT:

What? Now?

DEBS: *(sounding increasingly stern)*

No. With my husband.

MATT:

What, other than the thirty-year torrid love affair?

DEBS:

Oh goodness. I'm not worried about that. Keeps him out of my hair...
No... This idea of yours. What are you up to? He's acting all distracted –
I've not seen him so interested in anything like this for years.

MATT:

That's good, isn't it? It's just a project. I'm not sure where we're going
with it; but I thought you wanted him out of the house more.

DEBS:

So, you're claiming that it was MY idea now, are you?

MATT:

Yes! Pretty much! Last week when I was over for Sunday lunch... You
said he was being restless. You said he was getting under your feet, and
you wished he had a writing project on the go. Well, now he will. We're
working on it together.

DEBS:

But what is it, exactly?

MATT:

Well, it's not about my granny's old cat – if that's what you mean.

DEBS: *(chuckling)*

Ha! He told you about our conversation!?!

15

MATT:

He texted me this morning. You are a joker! Look – I'm hoping to get him out of a rut. We'll do this project together for a few months and it'll get his imagination working again and then he'll start coming up with new ideas of his own and then I can get back to my other projects too.

DEBS:

Ah! Well, I do hope my husband's not keeping you from your work!

MATT:

Not at all. I need a change of scene! Daft comedies about vampires do odd things to your brain. This is different! A spot of research on something factual and then we'll adapt it into something of our own.

DEBS:

I was wondering where that imagination you mentioned came into it. Oh well, you're probably right; just don't get him into trouble, please!

MATT:

I'll do my best. I promise.

DEBS:

Seriously now. What does this 'research' of yours actually entail?

MATT:

I'm not sure yet. Not until we start looking into it.

DEBS:

Hmm... Really? I'm not sure I believe you.

MATT:

I really don't know. You'll be the first we tell! Look, I've got to go –
I've a cat here who needs feeding. Catch you later, alright?

DEBS:

Alright. Bye for now. Thanks for reassuring me.

*(Matt puts down the phone and goes back to stroking Tolstoy. Back in
her home, Deb's still feels extremely wary about the whole matter)*

(Mutters) I'll be watching you Matt Spencer... I'll be watching you!

A WOMAN FOR ALL REASONS

EPISODE TWO: EMILY...

BY NICK GOODMAN

SCENE 4. INT. LIBRARY. EVENING.

(Early evening the same day. Matt and Bob enter their local Reference Library. Bob looks confused. Matt seems enthused; he stops short.)

BOB:

This isn't your section?

MATT:

No, it's the upstairs. We from downstairs folk are...well...we're looked down upon! We live with it – but deep inside we are crying.

BOB: *(chuckles in reaction)*

So, this is unexplored territory then?

MATT:

Bingo! That's her.

BOB:

That's who?

(Matt turns on his heel, heading for reception. He thumbs back to a studious-looking woman with frizzy hair; head down, glasses on nose.)

MATT:

Emily Bradnock! She knows you know!

BOB:

And what exactly does she know?

MATT:

I don't know. YET! *(awkward pause)* Let me show you. Sit down.

BOB: *(under his breath)*

Maybe a night in with Inspector Lambert would have been better…

(Matt grabs a book from a shelf and indicates that Bob should do the same. Bob randomly picks one called 'Hitler: The Final Moments', then sits, but flicks through the pages without even looking at them.)

This is the first one I found. Why the books? I thought we were here to talk to the girlie.

MATT: *(whispers)*

It's a calling code. Watch!

(Matt stands his copy of 'Arthur Askey: The McCarthy Letters' and peers over the top. After a while, Emily peers over towards them and lights up. She wanders over and sits with the boys. All her formality drains from her, and she reaches out a hand to Matt like a resentful prisoner being visited…)

EMILY:

You came back!

MATT: *(indicating Bob)*

This is Bob.

EMILY: *(holding Bob's startled hand)*

Bob, TELL HER STORY!

19

BOB: *(slowly)*

You what? Whose story?

EMILY: *(looking surprised – as if Bob is slightly stupid)*

Her! Miss Walsh!

(Bob looks at Matt trying to think fast and then he looks back to Emily.)

BOB: *(apologetically, to Emily)*

You're going to have to tell me more, I'm afraid.

MATT:

She doesn't know any more.

EMILY: *(excitedly)*

Matthew tells me you're a writer.

BOB: *(sounding sad)*

I was!

MATT: *(firmly)*

You are!

(To Emily) He is!!

EMILY:

So, you can dig and find, then tell us what you've found!? I am merely the rock you thrust aside as you plunged your hand in to reach for the treasure! I'm not quite sure how I feel about that, to be honest with you!

(Bob gulps, literary mystery far from his mind)

MATT: *(to Emily)*

We must know more.

EMILY:

Then meet me here at 1am

MATT: *(with an involuntary squeak of alarm)*

Hey!?! How are we meant to get in??!!

EMILY: *(producing a key)*

It's okay. I've already figured that out – it's not difficult; I'll just lock you in the stationary cupboard and let you out at the appointed hour.

BOB: *(clearly concerned that he'll get into trouble)*

I do have a wife at home, you know!!!

MATT: *(to Bob)*

She has her TV shows for company. But I have Tolstoy to think about.

EMILY:

Remember, to a cat, humans are pleasant but expendable company. He'll cope. Meet me at the cupboard at 7pm for lock down. Don't be late!

(Emily returns to her desk. Her manager, Neville, has grown a frown.)

BOB: *(to Matt)*

Why can't we just sit down and blow up spaceships like we used to. Is any research worth being locked in a cupboard for four hours!!!??

MATT:

This is going to be big. And it's real. She says so.

21

BOB: *(sarcastic)*

Oh, she says so. I'm sorry, but she's loop-de-loop old friend!

MATT: *(banging on the desk as quietly as possible)*

Exactly. A character like that is an essential part of any half-decent horror film and a few ropey ones too. Our plans are coming together!

BOB:

Matt! I wouldn't go that far. ALL we have is a name and a story. For that matter, we don't even have a story – just a request for a story.

MATT:

That girl has picked up loads of titbits from local sources, you know.

BOB: *(unhappy)*

Well... Okay... But why the cupboard??!! Why can't she just tell us?

MATT:

All the facts are scattered; she has no time to piece it together.

BOB:

But why can't she just set off the fire alarm and just get everyone out?

MATT:

Kirsten did that when she was tapping the Marquis of Hamilton; she's sweet on him, I think. She's now on her last warning with her manager.

BOB:

The mind boggles! It's a pity we weren't warned! What if we need the loo? My waterworks aren't what they used to be.

MATT: *(struggling)*

Thanks for that image. There are always the ink pots?

BOB:

Ugh! But they're full of ink!

MATT:

Cheer up. Live a little! Where's that Blitz spirit!?

BOB: *(holding his head in his hands)*

It's blitz-ed off! Hmm. It certainly gives a new meaning to getting a retainer. I wonder what old Inspector Lambert is doing now.

(Time passes. It is now 1am and all is quiet in the stationary cupboard. The door is unlocked. Inside, twisted at awkward angles and half asleep, Matt and Bob stir, moan, creak, stretch and blink before emerging from their 'tomb'. Fresh as a posy and dressed in burglar black, Emily leads them back to the Reference section. A power point projector stands ready. A sepia still of an old lady crossing a familiar medieval square is being projected.)

BOB: *(still bent over and bleary eyed)*

Oh dear... Not even in my youth did I do anything crazy like this.

(Emily clicks her fingers and indicates that the boys should sit. This they do, their offended backs reluctant to let them sit without a few creaks.)

EMILY: *(scooping up an indicator-stick she points it at the projection)*

Now then. Walsh! A local resident, as you can see. Outwardly a kindly old lady in unflattering stockings, although surprisingly pretty a good taste in fabulous hats.

(Turning to the boys, whipping glasses off and glaring)

23

Inwardly a dark enigma; with a bequest that has bank rolled the Boy Scouts, four local newsagents and The Mother's Union for 150 years!

BOB: *(non-plussed)*

Fancy.

EMILY: *(pointing her stick)*

Some say the brothel too!

MATT: *(shaking his weary head)*

This town has a brothel? I'm clearly out of the loop on this stuff!

BOB:

You and me both!

EMILY: *(sounding strict)*

Quiet! I'm not finished yet! Her name is associated with dozens of ventures – BUT *(slamming down her stick)* have you spotted what doesn't add up? Well!?

BOB:

She has all this cash but still couldn't afford decent stockings? Weird!

EMILY: *(impatiently)*

No!

MATT: *(more keenly)*

The Scouts didn't start until 1907!?

EMILY:

Good, but not quite....

(Emily zooms in on the picture using a remote control)

Behind Walsh is a Co-Op Advertising Green Shield stamps. I checked with the Marquis; his father was involved. That's the 1973 ad from nigh on fifty years ago!

(Matt and Bob try to reboot their tired brains. Emily sits wide eyed.)

If her bequest was 150 years ago, what was she doing walking around at liberty well over a hundred years later??!!

(Matt and Bob are briefly impressed. Then…)

BOB:

Are you sure it's the same person? This photo is definitely recent, right?

EMILY:

Yes! According to my sources, it is. I haven't left everything to you. I can show you the original; it's on the internet – long story, but that's where I came across it – it's all a bit hush hush as you can imagine!

MATT:

You're losing me. So, are you saying that she's the source of online gossip? What's to say that someone else isn't investigating this?

EMILY:

No… No… You're misunderstanding me… My attention was drawn because there seems to be a total security blackout on her.

MATT:

So, what we know is just in books? And this here photo? (*she nods*)

BOB:

So, what became of your helpful Marquis of Hamilton?

EMILY: *(Emily slumps back in her chair, she is solemn and thoughtful)*

He sloped off. Couldn't take the heat. Too close. Too much to lose!

(Turning to the boys)

So, there you are. It's up to you now! Good luck!

MATT:

You want us to look for clues in this library? At this time of night?

EMILY:

Whilst I catch up on my sleep. Yes please.

BOB:

…And after we've done that, you can let us out, right? We can go home?

EMILY:

Oh no – I'm afraid that won't be possible, the CCTV at the back door would give you away and pick you up leaving the building. Sorry guys!

MATT:

But haven't you got CCTV in the library here too?

EMILY:

Ah yeah – but it's switched off in here.

BOB:

Then why not just switch off the back door one!?

EMILY:

Unfortunately, that works off a master control. It's locked in Neville's office and only Neville has the key; for some reason he doesn't trust me!

MATT:

So, it's back to the cupboard after our labours, is it? That'll be fun!

EMILY:

Sorry! *(she scribbles on a post-it note)* You should try this guy; name of CB. I've never met him, but we have spoken at length, and he claims to be in contact with Walsh... *(eyes upwards)* If you know what I mean!

MATT: *(sounding sceptical)*

Is this more info from the Marquis?

EMILY: *(sounding increasingly sad as she continues)*

No, that tip off was from Billy... Poor Billy, I still regret everything that went on with him; but I'd need to be drunk to tell that story!

BOB:

Talking about drinking – I could really murder a coffee.

EMILY:

I've half a Fruit Shoot, if that'll help – the kitchen's locked, I'm afraid.

BOB: *(eyes closed)*

Another key that Neville doesn't trust you with. *(Emily gives a rather rueful grin but adds nothing more)* Never mind... Forget it! We'll cope!

27

SCENE 5: DEBS AND BOB'S LOUNGE. DAY

(Later that day. Matt is sat in a chair, Debs in another. He is fast falling asleep, an empty coffee cup rests in his lap; his head nods drowsily.)

DEBS: *(at the top of her voice)*

FIRE!!!

MATT: *(waking with a fright...)*

Where? What? Oh...

DEBS: *(giving a cheeky and somewhat satisfied grin)*

It's okay... No fire after all. I must have been mistaken.

MATT: *(grumpily)*

Don't do that! I have high blood pressure, you know!

DEBS:

Hmm... Well, now you're awake I think you were about to tell me why you kept my husband up all night without so much as a text.

MATT:

Yes, well there was no signal in the cupboard. Didn't Bob tell you?

DEBS: *(not best pleased)*

He did. He said exactly the same thing and it's not funny.

MATT:

Quite. It wasn't exactly a bicycle made for two I can tell you!! Look, I know what you're going to say next. What am I getting Bob into? Well,

28

I hear you, Debs – honestly, I do – but I'm too close to it. Too close yet still too distant to fully explain it, if you see what I mean.

DEBS:

No! No! I have no idea what you're going on about – I really don't!!

(Debs gets up, take Matt's cup, and goes to the kitchen to wash it...)

MATT: *(following her)*

You love a good mystery, don't you? Can't you see where we're at?

DEBS:

Mysteries just frustrate me! I'm a gore-hound; I love blood and bodies!

MATT:

I'm pretty sure that there will be some of that, too!

DEBS: *(turning)*

Just as long as it's not Bob who becomes a corpse!

MATT:

That'll never happen! This is an unexplained mystery, long hidden under motorways. With a little luck and research, we'll uncover it!

DEBS:

From inside a cupboard?

MATT: *(defensively)*

We were working undercover. I'll have you know.

DEBS:

Really. That's not really in my area of interest. I prefer grumpy detectives who can solve things because they are cleverer than everyone else. So, I don't have to think about it too much after a hard day at work. *(Matt looks increasingly out of arguments as fatigue kicks in. Debs looks thoughtfully, she pauses for a moment before continuing.)*

Okay, so where do we go from here?

MATT:

We carry on researching until we find out more. I know it won't be easy – but I think Bob is as into the whole project as I hoped he would be.

DEBS:

Yeah... I'd say so... You both seem pretty keen... But then what?

MATT:

Well, I thought it'd make a great TV show. I've always fancied doing a six-part mystery series – do you think Netflix would be interested? I mean, we'd both prefer the BBC – but Netflix is where the money is!

DEBS: *(pleasantly surprised, although sceptical)*

Ha! So, you hope it'll make you famous? What, really?

MATT: *(with a grin)*

Well Debs love, we HAVE waited a very long time to make it big!

DEBS:

What about me? Have you thought about that? *(Matt looks confused)* Think! Me. Fame. Have you thought about what'll happen to me; not just you and Bob? How are we all going to cope with His Majesty's finest gutter press crawling all over us. Is that really what you want?

MATT:

Oh look – I'm pretty sure that we can keep a low profile. I mean we've a lot of work to do before anything big might actually happen!

DEBS:

You need to think how all this could change our lives, Matt… Your life! Bob's! Mine! Poking around in all this might not unearth the treasures that you're hoping for – it may dig up something utterly unpleasant!

MATT:

You're exaggerating… It's an adventure… We'll be safe.

DEBS:

Don't pretend you've even thought about it beyond your next long night of research inside some random store cupboard… Neither of you have! It's all jolly japes to you! Bob's just as bad – but you're the ringleader!

MATT:

Come on, Debs. Don't be like that… We have thought about all this.

DEBS:

I thought you would have had more consideration. *(Suddenly irritable)* Go on, clear off. And, for God's sake, get some sleep!

MATT: *(placating)*

Look Debs, I...

(Debs heads quickly to the loo and slams the door. Gentle crying can be heard inside. Matt checks his mobile phone and sheepishly departs.)

SCENE 6: RAILWAY VIADUCT. NIGHT

(This is the stuff that horror films are made of... A dark, decrepit overgrown viaduct, with an old railway storage shed nestling below. Matt and Bob approach nervously. A lone light burns inside, whilst smoke wafts from the entrance and a hissing noise echoes from within.)

BOB:

Just think, 24 hours ago we were safely locked in a cupboard!

MATT:

Let's see this through. Just remember what Emily said. Plunge your hand in and grab the treasure!

BOB: *(wiping his brow)*

I was trying to forget that. She was young enough to be my daughter. I'm still an impressionable lad at heart.

MATT:

Come on then. We're asking for CB, right?

(Bob nods. Gingerly they enter the shed; the room ahead is festooned with techno-junk. It looks like an earthquake has hit. The source of the hiss is a large, primitive crystal radio on a table. Bob coughs loudly.)

BOB:

Hello? Anybody home?

(A head bobs up from a swamp of cable loops to reveal a jovial Kim Newman lookalike with glasses and a droopy moustache.)

CB: *(warily, but half-smiling despite the lit cigarette that he is smoking)*

Oh, hello there. You're not from the Council, are you?

BOB: *(sounding almost offended)*

Perish the thought!

CB: *(emerging from the cable jungle)*

Good. Only I'm kind of in limbo. Squatters rights at the moment; but I am hoping to come to a deal with our local station.

(Wiping his hand and offering it first to Matt, then to Bob)

And you are?

MATT:

Matthew… Call me, Matt… And this is Bob.

CB:

Oh right – nice – and are you lost?

MATT:

No… No… Emily sent us. Did she get a message to you?

CB: *(thinking)*

Emily? Who's Emily? I don't recall actually knowing an Emily…

BOB:

You ARE CB, aren't you? We're not in the wrong place.

CB:

Yes, I'm CB; so if it's me you want then you're spot on geographically!

MATT:

Well, that's a relief... By the way... CB... What does it stand for?

CB:

Jake Treherne.

BOB:

Shouldn't that be JT?

CB: *(laughing)*

No dummy! I'm a radio man *(Pointing to the crystal set)*

MATT:

Ham! *(CB looks confused)* It's a radio *HAM* isn't it?

CB:

Hey, I can assure you that I know exactly what I'm doing, thank you!

BOB: *(quickly)*

Yes... Yes... I never meant any offence... Err... Well now... You must have been in the business a long time by the look of your gear.

(Indicating the crystal set)

CB: *(proudly)*

That's Crystal. Isn't she lovely? We sit and hiss together most nights; occasionally French radio drifts in and serenades us. Awfully romantic!

BOB:

I take it visitors are not a frequent thing.

CB:

I've not forgotten how to entertain. Sit down. I'm making tea, would you join me? I've even got fresh milk and some sugar somewhere!

MATT/BOB:

Yes please!

(CB goes behind huge speakers and shuffles about some equipment...)

CB:

Come to think of it – you may have to wait a minute; I was actually repairing the kettle when you arrived. You aren't in any hurry, are you?

MATT:

Nah. It's fine – we can wait.

BOB: *(mouthing to Matt)*

There's nowhere so sit.

MATT: *(to Bob)*

Well, as this is a squat – lets squat!

(Both Matt and Bob sit cross-legged on the floor)

I've known you for thirty years and we've never tried so many positions as we have in the last 24 hours. Ha!

(Bob doesn't reply. He is staring with a look of fascinated confusion at the eruption of electrical flotsam jutting out from behind the speaker.)

MATT: *(to CB)*

Why have a next-to-useless crystal set? Everything is digital these days.

CB: *(from behind the speaker)*

Nobody ever thinks about this, of course, but when the radio world jumped on the Good Ship Digital, what happened to everything and everyone that got left behind? The shrapnel! That's what I look for.

BOB:

What about Walsh?

(CB urgently whips his head round the speaker, holding bits of kettle...)

CB:

How do you know about Walsh?

MATT:

Emily said you were in contact with her.

(CB becomes serious. He marches to the door, shuts it, and bolts it...)

BOB: *(eyes closed, fearful)*

Inspector, when you find my mutilated remains, I hope you'll spare my wife's feelings!

CB: *(CB squats level with his guests, he is suddenly smiling)*

It's no good saying "If I told you, I'd have to kill you!" Emily has already told you and she didn't bother; all very careless to my mind!

MATT:

So how do you contact her? Do you use a Ouija board or something?

CB:

Hell no. Superstitious mumbo jumbo! *(Pointing at the crystal set)*. It takes a Grand Dame to reach someone like Walsh!

BOB: *(scornful)*

Oh, come on. Are you telling me you can communicate with a ghost on all this war-time tat of yours? I'm sorry, I simply don't believe it.

(CB leaps up and puts the set's earphones over its loudspeaker...)

CB:

There, there Sweetie, he didn't mean it! *(To Bob)* When it comes to Walsh there are so many questions! Is she alive or dead? To be completely honest with you I don't know for sure.

(CB throws down the beyond-repair kettle testily at his guest's feet)

But since you have come here and invaded my space, you'll sit here, and you'll find out the answer right now as I do. Whether you like it or not!

(Matt and Bob look increasingly afraid. CB clicks the main light off and lights a candle in the dark, lighting the room. CB holds the candle in a vintage 'Wee Willy Winky' holder. He pushes it close to the boys.)

I'll teach you to meddle and scoff and demand tea from the dead!

(CB kicks the unfortunate kettle corpse once again and then slowly – apparently deep in thought – he removes the crystal earphones and adjusts the controls. Bob opens his mouth but then thinks better of it.)

Gentlemen, be careful what you wish for!

(Matt and Bob stare apprehensively at the old apparatus in the flickering candlelight and the hiss of the crystal set fills the room)

A WOMAN FOR ALL REASONS

EPISODE THREE: TRACING IN THEIR FOOT-STEPS...

BY PAUL CHANDLER

(Please Note: Events in episodes 2 & 3 occur at the same time... scenes 7 and 8 take place during the afternoon between scenes 5 and 6 and scene 9 takes place at night after scene 6.)

SCENE 7. INT. BOB'S HOUSE. AFTERNOON.

DEBS: *(sounding upset)*

Auntie, I'm sorry if I'm not at my most talkative today... I feel like I should have made plans; I just don't know where the morning's gone to!

ALICE: *(with sincerity)*

Don't apologise, dear. Anyway, you have the afternoon ahead of you... Where's that husband of yours? Not working from home today, I take it!

DEBS:

He's actually on a fortnight's leave.

ALICE:

Really!? You never mentioned going away. That'll be nice!

DEBS:

We're not – we can't afford it.

ALICE:

I'm sure that's not true. Honey, if you need a little loan – or an early birthday present then you know that I'm always good for it.

DEBS:

No, Auntie! It's really nice of you but I can't expect you to bail us out.

ALICE:

Nonsense! I told you it would be my treat – my absolute pleasure.

DEBS:

No. Really, Auntie. Thank you. It's my own fault. I need to get off my arse and find another job – Bob's been really good about it... so far!

ALICE:

Don't be so hard on yourself – I know things have been tough since you lost that job at the post office. Such a shame that place closed down; why they ever opened two so close to one another I'll never know.

DEBS:

I wish I could find a new job that interested me. It's just not happening!

ALICE:

You're being choosey about what you apply for; I don't blame you!

DEBS:

Neither does Bob – but sometimes I just wish he was a little more.

ALICE:

Bossy? Strict with you? Do you really?

DEBS:

I guess not. Bob's Bob and usually I make all the big decisions whilst he reads the newspaper and nods. Mostly I prefer that – like it, even.

ALICE:

But this time you could do with someone chasing you up about it more – well, I can do that for you, dear – I'll be sure to ring you every day!

DEBS:

Thank you, I really do think that might help.

ALICE:

But forget job hunting whilst Bob is off. You may not be able to have a holiday, but you can have days out, surely? What have you got lined up?

DEBS:

Nothing! Really... Nothing... We've not even discussed it.

ALICE:

Bob is happy to sit at home?

DEBS:

No. He's got a project of his own and he's off doing that.

ALICE:

So why aren't you here lunching with me, then? I'm literally sitting here twiddling my thumbs and counting the sparrows on my washing line!

DEBS:

Don't be silly, Auntie. You always have plans. I thought you were sorting through the jumble today for the church bazaar.

ALICE:

I am, dear – but I wouldn't say no to a helping hand.

DEBS:

Sorry, I should have offered; I could do with the distraction.

ALICE:

I knew there was more to this. What's wrong, love? Where is he?

DEBS:

Like I said, Bob is off out there researching with his pal, Matt.

ALICE:

The librarian? *(Debs mumbles something indiscernible)* Honey! What's going on? Those two can be trouble when they're together!

DEBS:

It's the early days of some joint writing project... Neither of them has clearly explained it – it's their little secret and it's getting me down.

ALICE:

They're not just off down the pub or at beer festival somewhere... This whole project thing might just be a way of covering it up.

DEBS:

I don't think so... I mean, I was grateful when I first heard about it... You know that Bob's been struggling with his writing for years.

ALICE:

His writing? You make it sound like a career; wasn't it only a hobby?
DEBS:

Auntie! It may have just been a hobby – but it's a big part of who he is.

41

ALICE:

Okay! So, Matt was going to do... what? Teach him how to write again?

DEBS:

Stop it!! It's not funny... You can't teach somebody how to write – but he was going to try and help... There was some story that he thought would make a good project for them both; I don't know more than that.

ALICE:

I see. So, where were they heading? To the library, maybe? To the pub to talk it out? I mean I don't exactly see a problem with that.

DEBS:

Only they were gone all night, Auntie.

ALICE:

You're kidding! What did they say about that? Late opening hours?

DEBS:

Something about a mystery... About getting locked into a cupboard and having no phone signal. They made it sound all very top secret.

ALICE:

Right. And you believe him? To be fair Bob is usually pretty honest about things like this – even if it doesn't paint him in a very good light.

DEBS:

Yes. Only...well, Bob never said a great deal about what happened. To be fair, he's been catching up with his sleep. It's more something that Matt told me that has been worrying me. In fact, I can't get it out of my head! Auntie, I really don't know what to think.

ALICE: *(sounding concerned)*

Well. If you're confused, then you need to wake Bob up and ask him what Matt meant. He might be cross that you woke him, but so what!?

DEBS:

I can't, Auntie! He's already up and he's gone out again.

ALICE:

With Matt? To do more of this so-called research?

DEBS:

Yes. He mentioned a 'site visit', but I really have no idea.

ALICE:

Then you need to get an idea. I mean it, seriously, dear... Deborah, my girl! You're your own worst enemy here! You need to do something!

DEBS:

I don't think I've the energy or the concentration to keep up with them!

ALICE:

Look, love, you need to be part of this, or it'll drive you two apart.

DEBS:

Oh no – Auntie, I don't think it will come to that.

ALICE:

But it might. No. You've got to make it clear. You need to be involved.
Look how anxious it's made you. What does Matt's wife say?
DEBS:

He's not married. He's single. To be honest, Matt doesn't seem very
interested in dating. He's always said that he's married to his writing.

ALICE:

How ridiculous! How pretentious for that matter. Listen, if you don't
know where they are then you're going to have to start at the beginning!

DEBS:

I don't get you. The beginning of what?

ALICE:

The beginning of the trail. Get thee to the library, Deborah. Find out
what they've been doing there. And why? And don't say you can't
because you jolly well can. Grab your coat. I'll be round in the car in
twenty minutes. We'll do this together. How does that sound? Good,
right. I could do with a bit of fresh air.

DEBS:

No... No! No! No!

ALICE:

I won't take that for an answer. I'm fetching my bag and I have my
keys. We'll sweep it all up into a shopping trip and a spot of coffee. It'll
be fun. You'll see. Get ready. I'm an unstoppable force.

DEBS:

AUNTIE!!

(BUT AUNTIE ALICE HAS RUNG OFF AND DEBS IS LEFT HOLDING A SILENTLY PURRING PHONE)

SCENE 8. INT. LIBRARY. AFTERNOON.

(No more than 45 minutes has passed since the previous scene – Debs reluctantly enters the library – she is as good as led by Alice – a tall woman who dresses precisely and wears a rather nice maroon hat that matches her dress, making her look like she is off to a garden party.)

ALICE:

Are you sure we're in the right part of the library, dear? It's very quiet.

DEBS:

Yeah, Auntie. It's a library. Library's usually are quiet.

ALICE:

Yes, I know that dear. So, who is it that we're looking to meet up with? Do you have any idea? A name? Anything?

DEBS;

Not really, no! You do know that I'm feeling very silly traipsing about like this. I swear the security guards were eyeing us up just now.

ALICE:

I think one of them may fancy me. I'm not bad for my age, dear. But what about you? Are you on their naughty list or something? Don't tell me you're banned from here? They didn't rescind your library card, did they? Oh, my goodness, they did!?!

45

(Pretends to be horrified – Debs just scowls)

Whatever did you do? Not... Not the old trouble again, surely?

DEBS: *(displeased)*

AUNTIE!! No... I've not wet myself since I was about four... *(mutters)* The old trouble... Really! I swear you enjoy embarrassing me.

ALICE:

I'm sorry! It's just that it's hard to forget; your mum would call me and...

DEBS: *(tersely)*

Yes... Thank you... But that hasn't happened recently, right!?

ALICE:

No... Fair enough... It's been a while! So... What DID you do?

DEBS:

I DIDN'T do anything!! My library card remains valid. I am NOT banned! I'm just having second thoughts about being here – on checking up on Bob and tiptoeing about like some cut-price Jessica Fletcher!

ALICE:

If it's any consolation, then you're a good decade off how old Jessica was on that show; I really wouldn't let it worry you. If Bob won't share all the details, then it's your job to find out the truth yourself!

DEBS:

Well, it's not that he's been lying to me.

ALICE:

Not that you know of. And at any rate it's hard to do when asleep.

DEBS:

Yes. Fair enough. I can't help but think the worst. I start theorising about what they're up to and then my imagination begins to work over-time. They're very secretive. It's not just Bob. Probably Matt has told him to keep it all to himself. It's just that it all sounds a bit ridiculous.

ALICE:

Probably because it is. So, do you know who it is we're looking for? You don't have to worry yourself, dear. I'll speak to him.

DEBS:

Her.

ALICE:

Her! Oh dear... How do you know it's a HER!?

DEBS:

I found a name and a number written in his desk diary.

ALICE:

And you rung it, I presume?

DEBS:

I did. And Emily picked up.

ALICE:

I hope you said it was a wrong number.

DEBS:

I was stuck for words – I just put the phone straight down.
ALICE:

Never mind. It's not the end of the world. Better than saying too much! So, this Emily. She works up here in the Reference Department, then? Which one do you think she is?

DEBS:

I don't actually SEE a librarian at the moment. Do you?

ALICE:

I do hope she's on duty after all this! I think perhaps we should just ask.

DEBS:

It just occurred to me – there may be another way.

ALICE:

Oh, yes? Do tell? Have you developed a sixth sense? That would help!

DEBS: *(impatiently)*

No, I'm serious! It's something that Bob had written by her name – the title of a book and I didn't understand it at the time. There was a big question mark by it. I'm wondering now if it wasn't some kind of code!

ALICE: *(confused)*

What ARE you going on about, love?

DEBS:

Help me find a book – 'Arthur Askey: The McCarthy Letters' to be exact!

48

ALICE:

Sorry? Excuse me? Are you making this up, dear?

DEBS:

No... Not at all. It must be here somewhere.

(One of the readers lets out an indignant "Shhhh!" and Debs and Alice lower their volume – searching the shelves in the media section where they presume the book will be, not noticing that they have company.)

VOICE: *(politely, but with a hint of impatience)*

Hello. Can I help?!

(Debs and Alice spin round – a librarian with short spiky hair and a KISS t-shirt is standing there, attempting to hide her displeasure at their arrival, but failing. Debs flounders and so Auntie Alice speaks up...)

ALICE:

Hello, my dear – two things... First things first – we're looking for a particular book. 'Arthur Askey: The McCarthy Letters'... I'm sorry, we don't know the author... *(turning to Debs)* Or do we, dear?

DEBS:

No, sorry. We do know that it's meant to be here in Reference though.

(The librarian, who they note from her badge is called Kirsten simply nods and beckons over to them)

KIRSTEN:

It doesn't sound like a reference work, but I think I know it. Follow me!

(They follow Kirsten; she seems to be leading them away from the books towards the Staff Only offices; Debs looks nervously at Alice.)

49

DEBS:

Where do you think she's taking us?

ALICE:

To the head honcho, I expect...

(Before Debs can say more, they arrive at their destination – Kirsten opens the door, sticks her head around and speaks to the occupant of the room before returning and ushering the ladies. As they enter, they see another lady who is busily cataloguing a pile of new library books.)

Emily, I presume? Nice office, by the way.

(The woman looks up smiling smugly and does not seem too surprised.)

EMILY:

Ah! Thank you! Wish it was mine – it's actually Neville's office – he's the boss up here – but he's away today.

DEBS:

Oh yes. I've heard Matt mention him.

ALICE: *(at a whisper)*

Did he say anything good?

EMILY:

I doubt it. There's nothing much nice to say, I'm afraid . Never mind, pleased to meet you. I take it that you're the wife?

ALICE:

No dear, not me. Her.

50

EMILY:

Sorry, I meant her.

DEBS: *(stepping forward)*

Emily, I don't want to waste your time, but I must ask something.

EMILY: *(ignoring her momentarily)*

By the way, I think I met your husband – Bob, wasn't it? Matt's friend.

DEBS:

That's the one... You locked them in a stationary cupboard too, I hear. That WAS true, I take it or did they just get drunk and pass out?

ALICE:

Was it some form of initiation ceremony? I don't understand that bit.

EMILY:

Not quite – but yes, it's true it did happen. They certainly didn't seem drunk. But I did lock them in there. It was necessary. Needed doing.

DEBS:

Are you sure? I'm not convinced myself. It seemed a bit over the top!

EMILY:

Oh, but a little drama can be fun. Gets people in the mood. I was under the impression that Bob needed some excitement – some adventure.

ALICE:

I do hope you were gentle with them, dear. They're easily bruised.

51

EMILY:

They're fine! Nobody manhandled anybody! Sorry, who are you, again?

DEBS:

Alice in the name. She's my Aunt...

ALICE:

Her FAVOURITE Aunt!

EMILY:

I never doubted it. Listen, I do hope you're not going to accuse me of kidnapping your husband – because I, most certainly, did not.

DEBS:

No. I know that. They came back to the house after they were here.

EMILY:

Presumably they don't know YOU'RE here? They didn't tell you much?

DEBS:

They don't and they didn't, no. They went out again this morning right after breakfast – and we want to know where you sent them.

EMILY:

Do you now?

ALICE:

Yes – this is why we're here. To find out what's going on.

EMILY:

I see. Well, I don't know if I can be bothered with the projector again. Believe it or not they're always threatening to limit the hours that we're allowed to have our lights on. It's bizarre, don't you think?

DEBS:

It is a bit strange – how are your readers meant to read?

EMILY:

I guess they're not – especially during the winter. They'd rather see us closed than using up their precious electricity and running up bills!

ALICE:

You'd think they'd be desperate to educate more people. We must have more stupid people in this world than ever. Look at Trump! Awful!

EMILY:

I'm not sure we've got time for that but thank you – you're quite right. Still, I'm glad we're all on the same score card with this one.

DEBS:

What's all this business about needing a projector? I don't understand!

EMILY:

Here! This pamphlet is exactly what I showed the boys on the screen!

(Debs takes the pamphlet, it contains the same sepia still of an old lady crossing a medieval square as had been projected for the boys earlier.)

Walsh! Outwardly a local resident with zero taste in fashion – inwardly – a dark enigma! She has a bank rolled the Mother's Union, four local stores and the local Boy Scouts for150 years! Etcetera... *(Emily yawns)*

53

DEBS:

I'm sorry. Are we keeping you up? Do you do this little talk a lot?

EMILY:

This is only the second time – maybe the third. But I do so hate going over the same territory all the time. Anyway – you read the pamphlet.

ALICE: *(taking it from Debs)*

Where did this actually come from? Is it something you give out here?

EMILY:

Of course not, no. I got one of my girls to knock this up the night your husband and his friend came here. We had a loose wire on the projector, so I thought I'd have to resort to print. In the end I didn't have to so they were never used. I was hoping I'd get a chance to use them. Here, Debs – have this... *(nodding to Alice)* You can keep that one.

ALICE:

So kind.

EMILY:

Now... Please... Read.

(There is a silence for a moment – it doesn't take the two ladies that long to read through it from end to end. Debs still looks confused, but Auntie Alice seems to have got the measure of the material)

ALICE:

Are you suggesting that this woman is... what? Eternal? Benefiting from some manner of elixir?

DEBS:

It would certainly appear that she's been around quite some time. Almost as long as you, Auntie.

ALICE: *(mutters)*

I'm writing you out of my Will.

DEBS: *(reflectively)*

I guess I deserved that one.

ALICE: *(turning back to Emily)*

So, let me see. The mystery here is two-fold. You suspect that this woman has been walking around for a good 150 years or more and it appears that someone – possibly her – has been doing their level best to keep anybody from finding out this fact. Even going so far as to somehow be wiping computer records that should be freely available on the Internet.

DEBS: *(whispers)*

You got all this from the pamphlet?

ALICE:

I did. I suspect that you just skimmed. You never were much of a reader. Your mother used to tear her hair out over it – but there was nothing that could be done. Anyway, I can assure you that it's all in there – very well researched and repackaged. Emily's team has done a good job at presenting the story in a precise manner. Your library training, no doubt!?

EMILY:

Something like that. I'd always intended to be a vet – but you can never be quite sure where life will lead you; now I tend to these tomes instead.
DEBS:

This is all very well and good – but where exactly does it get us?

EMILY:

You have a point. Listen – let's cut to the chase, shall we... I've got work to do and what might well be the beginning of one of my migraines. I'll give you CB's address same as I did Matt and his friend, your husband.

DEBS:

Bob.

EMILY: *(deliberately misunderstanding)*

No, thank you. I'll stay sat down, if you don't understand.

(Emily hands Debs a yellow post-it note with an address written on it in a pleasantly neat hand-writing, but Alice stretches forward and takes it first.)

ALICE:

Who's this CB, then?

EMILY:

Let's just say rumour has it that he's in contact with Lady Walsh.

DEBS:

In person or via a Ouija board?

EMILY:

Honestly, I don't know – if you find out then please do let me know. Should I call Kirsten – or can you see yourself out?

ALICE:

It's fine – we can see ourselves out.

(Emily sighs and puts a blindfold over her eyes and leans back in her chair.)

EMILY:

Thank you for calling. Farewell for now. Turn the light out when you go.

ALICE:

Turn the light out, dear, will you?

DEBS:

Sure. *(she does so)* I hope the migraine goes. Thanks again.

(But Emily does not reply, and Alice and Debs depart the office in silence.)

9. INT. VIADUCT. EVENING.

(Early evening the same day. Emily and Alice pull up in Alice's car by the railway viaduct, Alice is driving – Debs appears quite frazzled)

DEBS: *(sounding concerned)*

Auntie, I don't like this. Neither Bob or Matt are answering their phones and look where Emily's address has brought us – to this dump. What if she's behind all this. What if she's the culprit!

ALICE:

Calm down, dear. Culprit for what!? Nothing's happened yet. Also, I'm not getting any reception anyway. So, if Bob and Matt are in this area, they might be having the same problem.

DEBS:

So? What do you suggest we do – poke around under the viaduct until we find a hidden doorway through to some magical dimension?

ALICE:

Um... No... No, did I ever say that? That would be ever-so exciting, but also completely ridiculous. We can't see from the car – presumably there is a door or some such and we'll just knock on it and ask for Bob and Matthew.

DEBS:

Okay. Well, shall we just get on with it? It's getting dark. I don't want to be here for the Witching hour. We might both turn back into pumpkins.

ALICE:

I very much doubt it, dear. Why so nervous? I thought you wanted to know what was going on? We've come this far. You can always stay here.

DEBS: *(grumpily)*

NO! NO! IT'S FINE!! I'M COMING.

(Debs unbuckles her seatbelt and opens the car door – striding on ahead in an attempt to look confident and not at all concerned about events)

ALICE:

So glad to see you've changed your mind. Look now – I can see some sheds. Should we head for those? I can see a light. Looks like somebody is home. Maybe they'll do us a nice cup of tea. I must say I'm parched!

DEBS:

Are you serious? You really want to go over there?

ALICE:

You don't? Have you got the wrong shoes on again!?

DEBS:

It's not that. Actually... No... Let's be honest; it is that.

(Suddenly Debs loses her balance and falls into a patch of scrub that appears to be growing between the bridge and the shed)

Oh, dammit!

ALICE: *(turning back with concern)*

Oh, darling! Do you need a hand?

59

DEBS:

No! No, I'll be fine!

(She begins to pick herself up – then double-takes.)

OH! Auntie! Am I seeing things? Over there – a body! An actual CORPSE!!

ALICE: *(confused)*

Debs, love, what do you mean? Are you kidding?

DEBS: *(horrified)*

NO! NO! I'M NOT KIDDING!! LOOOOOK!

ALICE:

Okay! Okay! It's probably not real. Let me see.

DEBS:

AUNTIE... IT'S REAL... IT'S REAL...

(Alice hurries over – Debs is already on her feet – staring in horror and backing away. Alice draws close – looking down with some reluctance at the shape that Debs is indicated, she shakes her head, muttering fearfully)

ALICE:

I don't believe it. This can't be happening.

A WOMAN FOR ALL REASONS

EPISODE FOUR: "IF YOU GO DOWN TO THE WOODS TODAY..."

BY NICK GOODMAN

(Please Note: Scene 10 takes place between scenes 8 and 9. From therein events continues from the cliff-hanger to scene 9)

SCENE 10. INT. REFERENCE LIBRARY. NIGHT

(Emily is locking up the library, logging off computers and turning off lights. She picks up one of her pamphlets. She stares at the picture of Walsh, touches it, and then flinches as if shocked or surprised. A work-deadened Kirsten trudges into the Reference library, iPod earphones in her ears.)

KIRSTEN:

Cheers then, Em. See you Friday.

EMILY: *(Tapping her pamphlet she rounds on Kirsten)*

One moment... *(she pauses)* What are you doing this evening?

KIRSTEN:

'Bake Off' I suppose.

EMILY:

And?

KIRSTEN:

White Lightning. Maybe a curry...

EMILY:

Catch it on I-player. 'Bake Off', I mean. And I'm pretty sure you can have that curry another night.

KIRSTEN: *(confused)*

Huh? I don't get you.

EMILY:
I need your help.

KIRSTEN:

I haven't got any money.

EMILY:

I've just paid you!

KIRSTEN:

That's only cos Neville's off.

EMILY:

It's the same money, girl. Look, I need to go and check something. It's all to do with that big project I mentioned to you. Remember?

KIRSTEN:

But you said you had two crazy blokes helping you do that.

EMILY: *(pulling on her coat)*

Yes. I've been thinking. Those two pitching up has changed things. *(Kirsten looks blank)* The ones you brought to me. Mrs Matt and the old girl.

KIRSTEN:

Oh yeah. Sorry. Yeah, I remember. What about them?

EMILY:

They were going after Matt and Bob. Too many people are muscling in on this. Maybe it's time I got a piece of the action – or at least watched it.

(To Kirsten) Come on.

KIRSTEN:

Must I go? Really?

EMILY:

Yes. REALLY!?

KIRSTEN:

What about my Mum?

EMILY:

No, just the two of us.

KIRSTEN:

No, I mean what do I TELL her?

EMILY:

Text her.

KIRSTEN:

She'll KILL me!

EMILY:

Then ensure you have witnesses for your demise. Because its witnesses we need. Witnesses like you and I. Now come on!

(Emily departs. Kirsten follows, none too happy...)

SCENE 11. EXT. VIADUCT AND WOODS. NIGHT.

(As before. Debs and Alice are stood over the huddled, faced down body)

DEBS: *(trying to remain composed)*

What the hell do we do? We can't just leave it!

ALICE:

Have you thought it might be Matt or Bob? At least turn it over and see.

DEBS:

I can't do that! Maggots and everything. Bleurgh! Surely it can't be them.

(The door to CB's shack crashes open, a fierce radio oscillation is heard. Over it, Matt's insistent hissing voice)

MATT:

Debs! Get away from him!

(Matt and Bob emerge from the shack, rather surprisingly they are on the ground rather than standing upright and begin slowly wriggling towards Deb and Alice, their lamp flame spluttering in the night breeze)

ALICE:

Thank God for that. What are you doing down there?

BOB:

Quiet! Don't wake him up!

DEBS:

Who?

MATT:

It's a long story. Now get away from him.

DEBS: *(now irritated)*

You and your bloody mysteries!! Stop this at once!!

(Before Alice can stop her, Debs turns over the body. The muddied, Kim Newman-esque face of CB is revealed...)

So, who the hell is this? *(To Matt and Bob)* What have you done??!!

BOB:

It's CB.

ALICE:

Oh, I was expecting someone in a suit.

DEBS:

Auntie please!

(CB's eyes snap open and he exhales heavily. Debs shrieks and jumps up. CB reaches out for her)

MATT: *(Getting to his feet)*

Get into the woods, all of you!!!

(Matt, Bob, Alice, and Debs all run into the adjacent foliage. The candle held by Bob finally gives out, plunging them into moonlight only. They look out to see CB stalking towards the entrance to the shack)

CB:

I know you're out there! I know what you want, and you can't have it!!!

BOB: *(mutters)*

All we asked for was tea!

ALICE:

Nice company you keep boys!

BOB: *(to Debs and Alice)*

What are you doing here?? It's dangerous!

DEBS:

That's why we came. What have you got yourselves into?

MATT:

If you'd only given us longer then we'd have found out what we were after.

BOB: *(flustered)*

How did you even find us?

ALICE:

Emily! Now there's a Minx. She sent you down here I understand.

(CB is now strutting about outside the shed and growls like an animal)

To that freak!

MATT:

Geek, not freak. He just collects radio bits. He's harmless really!

DEBS:

But look at him! I know there's a moon tonight but that's milking it!

BOB:

We only asked him a question!

ALICE:

What happened to him? Why was he lying on the ground like that!?

MATT:

We haven't got a clue! Honestly, we haven't. It's a mystery!

DEBS: *(still in shock, 'shouting' in low tones at Matt)*

What have you got my Bob into??! I leave you both alone for a couple of nights and its being locked in cupboards by mad women and now this!!!

(Everyone shushes Debs. CB turns sharply in their direction...)

CB: *(voice now plummy)*

Thieves! Teach you to scrump on my land. Sabre! Titan! See them off!

(Fierce barking is heard, slavering, panting, crunching of undergrowth.)

ALICE:

Dogs!?!

BOB:

Where did they come from? He was totally alone when we were in the shed.

MATT:

Who cares, let's get moving.

(CB is strutting about like a sentry, giving the Scouting "Dib Dib" salute.)

CB: *(speaking to himself, to them, to the night)*

IS NOTHING SACRED?!?

(Alice, Debs, Bob, and Matt crash through the forest in near pitch darkness. As they stumble through, they keep their dialogue going)

DEBS: *(sounding concerned)*

I can't see a damn thing. Stay close to me, Auntie.

BOB:

Honestly, Debs why did you have to go and spy on me like this? Now you're both in this mess too? Is there really no part of my life I can keep to myself?

ALICE:

Don't you have a go at Debs. She was worried sick about you, sitting there at home by herself on your holidays. It's a good job that I came to help her.

BOB:

If you two hadn't interfered.

ALICE:

You and Matthew would be cowering in that shed in fear for your lives!!

MATT:

Instead of which we are running from dogs in fear of our lives!!

ALICE:

Dogs just don't have any manners these days. I fear all that hard work done by Barbara Woodhouse back in the 1980s has come to nothing.

MATT: *(hitting something)*

OWW!! *(pause)* Oww again; I've hurt myself by the way!

BOB:

Where are you? I can't see you in these shadows.

MATT:

Hanging over a log, I think. Whatever it is I walked smack into it. It hurt!

BOB:

Everybody just stop for a moment! We need to get our bearings.

DEBS:

Oh hell, you'll be lucky to get anything – its pitch black out here!

69

BOB:

Talk to me, Matt. I'll follow your voice. Let me know when I'm close.

MATT: *(singing)*

"Mooooove closer. Move your body real close…"

DEBS:

Oh, get a room, boys!

(Someone's phone goes off. Bob answers. It must be Bob's)

BOB: *(sounding quite annoyed)*

Hello… yes? Oh… Right. It's you. Look, Mr Whittaker – I did tell you that I wasn't working tonight! I usually have Wednesday nights off anyway – but I'm actually meant to be on annual leave this week on top of it! So, will you not ring me again, please? Yes, I'm sorry too.

(Bob hangs up)

No delivery drivers tonight so guess who gets called at this hour! Typical! Are you okay now Matt? Nothing broken, I trust?

MATT:

Not that I'm aware of. I'm okay. Look Bob, I've been thinking

ALICE:

A little late in the day for that…

MATT:

What actually HAS happened to CB?

BOB:

He's become a lunatic from looks of it – I'm not sure I'm equipped to give an exact medical diagnosis. So, I'm afraid that will have to do for now!

MATT:

But why?

BOB:

Well, it must have been the séance.

DEBS:

Hey look! My watch illuminates if you press this. I can't believe we're sat here in a bush – it's gone midnight, you know; we should be drinking cocoa.

MATT:

You're over-playing it a bit, Bob. Ladies! There was no séance! He just lit a candle, turned out the lights and switched on the radio.

BOB:

Maybe that's all it takes. The mysterious ways of the supernatural.

ALICE:

Let's get a move on, fellas. I can hear those yappers approaching again…

MATT: *(hitting into Bob)*

Ouch! Sorry Bob, you were closer than I thought.

(Everyone starts moving off again only slower, Matt turns to Bob)
Seriously, what is he doing? Growling, prowling, marching. He isn't

71

exactly channelling an old woman. There is a rational explanation somewhere.

BOB:

Well thank you, Richard Dawkins!

MATT:

Hey?! What's that supposed to mean?

BOB:

It does seem a bit of a shame you know. We have spent decades writing about aliens, monsters, pirates, ghosts, fairies...

MATT: *(hurriedly)*

You wrote about fairies, mate! I had nothing to do with that one!

BOB:

...And the moment we get something that is beyond our ken, you come over all RATIONAL! What happened to the Matt, I knew – are you an alien clone?

MATT:

All I'm simply saying is that it doesn't make sense. The dots don't join up.

ALICE:

Will you two keep it down!?! You're yapping more than those doggos!

DEBS:

Look over there! We're reaching the end of the woods. There's a bridge!

72

ALICE:

Thank Heavens. I'm quite a fit old bird even if I do say so myself – but I have to admit all this running was killing me.

(The group can now just about see each other in the moonlight)

MATT: *(grabbing Bob)*

Of course! The radio!!

BOB:

Come again?

MATT:

Ultrasonics. Some kind of signal that set him off.

BOB:

How can we prove that, Professor?

(Debs and Alice hug each other as they reach the clearing)

ALICE:

You do realise, love, that it's a pretty long walk back to the car

(They all run across to the bridge and start mounting the steps up to it)

BOB: *(calling after them)*

Well, if Einstein here is right, we need to go back through the woods the other way to get us back to the hut.

DEBS: *(dismayed and very much anti the idea)*

Hey? What! Are you crazy? This is our best chance to get into the streets and get home! What about the dogs? What about our oafish pursuer?

BOB: *(smiling, catching on)*

What dogs? We heard noises but we never actually saw them, did we?

(Reaching the top of the bridge, Bob looks down towards the forest)

Look down there.

(Debs and Alice do indeed look)

MATT: *(to Debs and Alice)*

No barkers! No actual woofs of any kind for that matter.

BOB: *(to himself)*

Hmm… That'll be your actual ultrasonics. Just you see!

SCENE 12. INT. BADGER WATCH ENCLOSURE. NIGHT

(Dressed in black, Emily is sat in a badger-watch encampment which has long been abandoned. She is looking through an observation hatch with binoculars. Kirsten is behind her, cold and depressed wearing a short coat and a woolly hat. She is examining the walls. There is a damp and puckered up photocopied picture of a dead badger sellotaped to one wall; below it is the melted remains of a candle)

KIRSTEN:

Oh, look Em. Poor little badger.

EMILY: *(without turning round)*

There is nothing little about a badger, young Kirsten. They're ginormous!

KIRSTEN:

Is this where people used to watch them at night?

EMILY:

Correct. Until the last cull. That's how I knew about this place. From the Marquis. A perfect spot to keep our own watch.

KIRSTEN:

Did he watch them?

EMILY:

No, he organised the cull.

KIRSTEN:

Heartless bastard.

EMILY:

Correction, gutless bastard. Hamilton ran out on me. Unlike these little heroes. Now, do be quiet.

(Kirsten joins Emily at the hatch)

KIRSTEN:

Have you actually seen anything yet?

EMILY:

Oh yes.

KIRSTEN:

And?

EMILY:

Tantalising. But I was right to bring us down here. The women have arrived. Matt and Bob launched into the wood like the Devil himself was after them. Can't see why. And over there, I perceive, is CB himself!

KIRSTEN:

CB? Who is that, exactly?

EMILY:

Keep up, child. The character that I sent them down here to meet.

KIRSTEN:

Looks like it didn't pan out so well. Can I have a look?

(Emily passes the binoculars to Kirsten)

What the F…???

EMILY:

Quite.

KIRSTEN:

What's he doing?

EMILY:

Marching. A spot of saluting too for good measure.

KIRSTEN:

Nice! What's that noise he's making?

EMILY:

'The Happy Wanderer'. It's the traditional anthem of the Boy Scouts.

(Struck by a thought)

Boy Scouts!

(Fishing out her pamphlet)

Walsh! Scouts! That could be a clue.

(Snatching the binoculars back and looking out of the hatch once more)

Exciting, isn't it?

KIRSTEN: *(pulling down her hat and crossing her arms)*

No, it's fecking boring! You've got another hour then I'm pissing off, boss or no boss. And stop calling me "girl", or "child" or "young". That's Granny talk. You're probably only a bit older than me.

EMILY: *(still glued to the CB scenario)*

Two years, nine months, and four days to be precise. According to your record card. The joys of a photographic memory.

KIRSTEN:

Hmm. How did you know that's CB? You told me you hadn't met him.

77

EMILY:

Well, that is the shack I sent them to. Elementary dear Kirsten!

KIRSTEN:

Listen, I'm scared Em. He looks a real nutter.

EMILY:

Just hold it together and we can be at the centre of a real wow. That will get you noticed more than your spiky hair. At the moment the only kiss you get is on your t-shirt.

KIRSTEN:

That's harsh even for you, Em. You don't know the half of what I get up to in my spare time! Anyway, your mad lot have pushed off. Why can't we?

EMILY: *(slightly more affectionately this time)*

How about you save it for your autobiography.

KIRSTEN:

You bet I will. Look, why are you so obsessed with this CB guy?

EMILY:

Look at him. He's expecting them to come back. I know Matt will want to know more. They ARE coming back, I guarantee it. Something else has to happen before the night is done and I must know what!

(Kirsten yawns. It is way past her bed-time)

78

SCENE 13. EXT. SHACK. NIGHT

(Matt, Bob, Debs and Alice are now in 'Famous Five' mode. Matt's theory has galvanized them all and they are no longer tired. They edge round the back of the shack. Strains of 'Jerusalem' can be heard, as sung by CB)

MATT: *(whispering to the others)*

We slip past him. First me, then Bob, then Debs. Alice, this could be dangerous. I dunno. Do you want to keep look-out just in case?

BOB:

Stay here Auntie. I'd never forgive myself if something happened to you.

ALICE:

Rubbish. Neither of you know how to fight off this weirdo. You need me.

DEBS:

Never mind about ME being in danger!

BOB: *(to Debs)*

Okay, you stay here, and we'll take Auntie.

DEBS:

I'd never forgive myself if something happened to Auntie.

MATT:

Oh, for Heaven's sake, no one is hitting anyone. We are just going to slip past behind him, turn of his radio and break the connection. Right?

DEBS/MATT/ALICE:

Right!

(They all move round the front of the shack, Debs and Alice one side, Matt and Bob the other. CB stands like Britannia, faced away from the shack, singing the last verse of 'Jerusalem', unaware his guests have returned. As Bob enters the shack his foot hits the ubiquitous dead kettle. CB swings round to confront them)

CB:

Oh no you don't! My favourite channel. There's no I-Player for this show!

MATT: *(at the radio)*

Bring back 'Closedown', that's what I say.

(Matt defiantly clicks the radio off and the crackling stops. CB gasps and slumps to the ground.)

ALICE: *(looking down at CB)*

This one could definitely have benefited from a dose of National Service. Anti-social lay-about. Although he could yet be redeemed.

MATT:

Enough of the personal comments. We did bring all this on ourselves.

(CB wakes groggily. Matt goes to help him. Alice goes over to the crystal set and looks at it thoughtfully)

CB:

What the hell happened? What time is it?

(Touching his face and noticing his mud-encrusted moustache)

I've really got to change the filter on that kettle!!!

DEBS:

Good luck finding a filter in this lot.

(Suddenly alarmed)

Auntie, what are you doing? Move away from that!

(Alice suddenly turns the radio back on and adjusts the setting)

ALICE:

It's alright, it's another channel. I just want to try something.

CB: *(to Alice)*

Hey, what are you doing to Crystal?

(A new warble – like a form of Morse code – emits from the radio)

ALICE: *(with a knowing smile)*

You're out there somewhere. I know you, don't I? There's no use hiding.

(Everyone is transfixed at this turn of events – they look at one another questioningly. What does it all mean!?)

A WOMAN FOR ALL REASONS

EPISODE FIVE: WATCHING... LISTENING IN...

BY PAUL CHANDLER

SCENE 14. INT. BADGER WATCH ENCLOSURE. NIGHT

(Emily and Kirsten are still watching from the badger enclosure. Emily clearly isn't getting the results that she wants. Kirsten is beyond bored)

KIRSTEN:

So, how long does this movie go on for, exactly?

EMILY:

Movie! What movie!?

KIRSTEN:

Sorry. I keep forgetting that this is actually happening in real-time.

EMILY:

You're a child of Netflix – this is the trouble. Think of this as your very own reality TV show – but without all the big prizes at the grand finale.

KIRSTEN:

At least nobody will be releasing a dodgy album of cover versions at the end of this one. At least I hope they won't.

EMILY:

I wouldn't bet on it! I don't trust anyone under 40 not to try and release an album of cover versions to compliment any random event.

KIRSTEN:

Hey! I'm under 40! For that matter I'm under 30. Just so, don't be mean!

EMILY:

When's the album out?

KIRSTEN:

That's not fair – I've never even heard of that being a thing.

EMILY:

Oh, I have. I went to a birthday party for a niece of mine recently and they'd done exactly that. My brother-in-law had recorded an album of him and his friends playing some of my niece's favourite songs on an acoustic guitar with a bongo drum accompaniment.

KIRSTEN:

Oh! You're kidding! Some people have no shame. Really?! Wow!

EMILY:

No... I lied... *(she pauses)* I'm being sarcastic; it actually happened!

KIRSTEN:

Okay! I'm sorry – I didn't mean to doubt you! That does sound awful. What kind of songs were there?

EMILY:

Mainly awful ones. The kind of thing that a three-year-old would like...

KIRSTEN:

That's weird. And how old is your niece?

EMILY:

She's three.

KIRSTEN:

Oh...

EMILY:

But that's not the point. The point is that people do these ridiculous over- blown things for events that really aren't particularly important at all.

KIRSTEN:

Like your niece's third birthday.

EMILY:

Sure. You probably think I'm harmless, but I do have a point! It's important to the girl – to her parents clearly and I suppose it's nice enough for everyone else who was invited. Although the birthday cake was far too dry.

KIRSTEN:

I hate dry birthday cake.

EMILY:

Oh, me too. Nothing worse... Well, there is – but nothing worth talking about anyway. I won't give examples, or we'll be here all day.

KIRSTEN:

Hey! Why not. It appears we actually HAVE all day!

EMILY:

Don't exaggerate. Listen, all I'm saying is – if, when you were three, your father and his friends had gone so far as to record an album of all your favourite kiddy tunes then wouldn't you have grown up to think that you were somehow very special. Wouldn't you expect the rest of the world to spoil you accordingly? Wouldn't you grow up to believe that you were entitled to something MORE? Just think about it. It's a slippery slope to a life of egomania and potential Trump-like Messiah complex.

KIRSTEN:

I really can't say I can't remember anything from back when I was as young as three. Oh, and I'd rather you didn't say the T word in front of me.

EMILY:

Apologies. It just came out. Anyway, that's getting off the point. I mean, how many three-year olds get treated that way? It must affect them.

KIRSTEN:

It sounds like it was more about her father wanting to get the chance to record an album – to give him more of an excuse to hang out with his mates and mess about with guitars.

EMILY:

Hmm. You could be right. My sister can be a bit of a chore to live with.

KIRSTEN:

I suppose it depends whether this is a one-off. The whole album business. If it just happens that once, then maybe it's nothing more than a rather sweet piece of fun. But if he does it every year then, yeah. Maybe it might leave you presuming that you're a little bit more special than most kids.

EMILY:

Exactly my point. What next? A movie? A party in The Royal Albert Hall!? Actually, I'm surprised this hasn't happened already. My brother-in- law is kind of bonkers but then I really do think that my sister is largely to blame for all this. Goodness knows what they'll do if she ever gets married. Hold the reception up on Mars, with cute Martians in tuxedos.

KIRSTEN:

Probably. That would be awesome. Could I be your plus one for that, please?

EMILY:

Kirsten, are you actually listening?

KIRSTEN:

Kind of half-listening. Half deciding that what could possibly be going on down in that shack might actually be more interesting to concentrate on than listening to you talk about your niece and her plans for world domination. I genuinely concerned that my ears may start bleeding in a minute!

EMILY:

You do realise that I'm your boss. You're being quite rude.

KIRSTEN:

Outside of work you're not my boss and don't even think about taking this out on me next time we do a shift together. You should be paying more attention. Something odd is happening down there. Have a look.

EMILY:

I will do – when I'm ready.

KIRSTEN:

Fine! Hey, you don't carry air freshener with you, by any chance?

EMILY:

Err, no. Why would I do that?

KIRSTEN:

It's just so badger-y in here. Can't you smell it?

EMILY:

It doesn't bother me – it reminds me of an Uncle of mine.

KIRSTEN:

Your Uncle was a badger?

EMILY:

No, stupid. He used to collect them.

KIRSTEN:

He collected badgers?

EMILY:

China ones, yes.

KIRSTEN:

Someone has to, I guess! Hey, something's definitely going on down there!

EMILY:

What? Okay, budge over – I'm ready now. Give me a go with the telescope.

KIRSTEN:

I just saw a car drive up. It was dark, and the doors haven't opened yet.

EMILY: *(taking the telescope)*

Oh yes. I see what you mean. What a battered old piece of tin. Hmm... looks like they have visitors, but I wonder who it is?

KIRSTEN: *(casually)*

Want to go find out?

EMILY: *(surprised)*

What do you mean?

KIRSTEN:

I'm fed up of hiding away up here. I want to hear every word and sadly we just can't afford to bug the place. My hearing really isn't up to it!

EMILY:

You're right! You're right. I forget you don't lip-read. Hmm...what about these new arrivals? Who do you think they are?

KIRSTEN: *(thoughtfully)*

I dunno. Let's just be careful – it's hardly going to be The Mafia, is it?

EMILY:

Nope. Although it could possibly be worse.

KIRSTEN:

What could be worse than The Mafia.? Other than Donald Trump.

EMILY:

Now who's using the T-word. Don't even joke about it. Come on!

(The two of them head out from where they have been hiding and their voices die away as they depart)

SCENE 15. INT. SHACK. NIGHT

(Down by the shack – Bob, Matt, Debs and Alice are crowded around the radio which is still emitting a Morse code style warble. It seems to have quite a hypnotic effect on CB and a rush of emotions seem to flood through him. Matt and Bob eventually break away and are trying to tidy some of the mess made earlier by CB whilst he was swirling around to the sounds)

DEBS:

Auntie – are you going to tell me what all this means? You seem to have some idea – or am I reading into all of this?

ALICE:

No, no dear. You're not far wrong. Let's say I know but I don't know.

DEBS:

That makes absolutely no sense at all, Auntie.

ALICE:

Well, I know there's some kind of message being transmitted. But I can't honestly say I understand what the message is or who is sending it.

DEBS:

Clearly not CB as he's sitting there looking enthralled.

ALICE:

You're right, Debs. You are. Although I suspect he may know more than we do. He may know who is sending the message. He may even know what they're saying.

DEBS:

And maybe he'll tell us.

ALICE:

Maybe he will – or maybe we can work it out for ourselves.

DEBS:

I can't keep up with you, Auntie. I thought you said you yourself thought you knew who was communicating this message.

ALICE:

Well, yes. I think I do. That doesn't mean for sure I know exactly who it is. There are things... things that are coming back to me. This all happened a very long time ago. I'm vague about it. But I intend to remember.

DEBS:

Are you sure you don't know more than you're saying?

ALICE:

Quite sure. I know it must be sounding quite mysterious to you, but I'm saying as much as I'm remembering. I suppose that's different, isn't it?

DEBS:

It is a bit, yes.

ALICE:

Never mind, aye. Do you have your phone with you?

DEBS:

I do, yes.

ALICE:

If I remember rightly, it's one of those modern ones, isn't it? Very nice. An iPhone, right? Presumably it has voice memo.

DEBS:

It does. I know that for a fact as I have a voice memo pal in Australia.

ALICE:

A voice memo pal?

DEBS:

It's like a pen pal. Back in the day we used to send each other audio tapes of us chatting – with music interspersed. Anyway, now we occasionally send voice memos, instead – it's all just a bit of fun, but we enjoy it.

ALICE:

Why ever don't you just Skype each other?

DEBS:

We do. Around our birthdays and at Christmas. But she's always so busy. I lose track of how many kids she has. And then there's the time difference!

ALICE:

Alright dear, if it makes sense to you. So, where's this phone, then?

DEBS:

Oh... You want it?! Who are you going to call?

ALICE:

Nobody dear. I just want to record a sample of this Morse code that is coming out of this here radio. It could prove useful to our investigations!

DEBS:

Oh! Golly... Yes... Sure...

(Debs gets out her phone and then quickly but carefully passes it over to her Aunt, indicating where the voice memo can be accessed. Alice activates it and the whole room falls quiet whilst she records)

CB:

Fascinating! Fascinating!

ALICE: *(distracted, beginning to record)*

That's enough of that. *(stopping it)* Email it to me, will you?

DEBS:

Sure...

ALICE:

Now, I mean. Just to be sure.

DEBS:

What's the rush. It's on my phone.

ALICE:

But if you lose your phone. Two copies are better than one.

DEBS:

Oh. Fair enough. It won't take a second. *(she takes the phone, clicks on a couple of things, types her email address and sends it)* Done!

ALICE:

Thank you! Sorry, love, didn't mean to be bossy.

(Debs nods and is about to speak, but then C.B. interrupts.)

CB:

Fascinating! Fascinating! FASCINATING!!

DEBS: *(whispers)*

Do you really think he understands the code? Maybe he's just gabbling.

ALICE:

Yes. Maybe. I think he does. *(turning to address CB)* Well? You do understand it, don't you? Are you going to tell us what it's all about?

CB: *(guardedly)*

Can't do that. It's top secret.

(At this moment Bob comes hurrying over. He looks a little flustered)

BOB:

We have company.

DEBS:

Tell them to go away, then. I don't think CB is up to visitors.

BOB:

I'm not sure they'll listen.

ALICE:

Oh dear. Let me speak to them. Who are they?

MATT:

It's actually us that they want to speak to us, as it happens.

(Alice and Debs look up – CB remains oblivious. Matt and Bob are standing in the doorway and behind him are two policemen)

ALICE: *(smiling cordially)*

Oh. Just in the nick of time officers, I have a favour to ask. Will one of you kind gentlemen please help me up? I'm not as nimble as I once was.

(The policemen look confused, but one of them steps forward to help. Debs, Matt and Bob look on in some astonishment, whilst CB appears to have fallen into some kind of trance – quietly muttering away to himself)

SCENE 16. INT. LOCAL POLICE STATION. NIGHT

(Matt, Bob, Alice and Debs are waiting in a holding room in the local Police Station. They are confused, but at least they have tea! Nobody speaks.)

BOB:

What happened to the actual Police? They seem to have forgotten us.

MATT:

Who knows! So, are we under arrest? And if so, what for? Trespassing?

DEBS:

I don't think so. By the way, they never actually said we were under arrest.

ALICE:

Yes, they just said that they had some questions.

BOB:

Where do you think they took old CB? I hope they don't think we were having some kind of drug-fuelled party in that shack.

DEBS:

Why EVER should they think that,for goodness sakes? I don't even have so much as a vitamin pill on me!

MATT:

Well, to be fair – CB did look a little out of it.

DEBS:

Maybe, but that's nothing to do with us. Let them do a test. I'm drug free!

ALICE:

Yes, dear, as far as I know we all are.

BOB:

I am! What about you, Matt? Did you have your morning bowl of drugs today or have you moved on to something more esoteric?

MATT:

Dammit – I knew I'd forgotten something.

ALICE:

No need for sarcasm, boys.

DEBS:

Thank you, Auntie. We wouldn't be in this mess if it wasn't for you two.

BOB:

Well, that's not very nice.

MATT:

I was trying to encourage him To give him something to write about!

DEBS: *(crossly)*

Well, you certainly succeeded there. Are you allowed crayons in jail? Because the way you're going, you're not going to be using a computer.

ALICE: *(attempting to soothe tempers)*

I doubt it will come to that. Also, you must admit – it is interesting.

DEBS:

Oh Auntie! Don't encourage them!

(At that moment the doors open, and a Police Officer stands in the doorway)

OFFICER:

Right. You can go home.

DEBS:

At last! This just isn't good enough We've not done anything wrong! You've kept us waiting quite long enough; you've not even questioned us!

BOB:

Thank goodness. I need to get back. Tonight's bath night, you know.

OFFICER:

I wasn't addressing you all. Ladies follow me! Gents to the front desk, please!

BOB:

Just a minute! You can't split us up like this.

ALICE:

Don't worry, Bob, she's with me! They may just need us to sign something!

MATT:

Hmmm… I don't much like the sound of this.

OFFICER:

Just be grateful that we didn't leave you to stew overnight. Ladies, this way, please. We want you to answer some questions. It won't take long.

(Debs and Alice are led away, leaving a bemused Matt and a distressed Bob)

ALICE:

But where are you taking us? What about the boys? I don't mean to be rude, Officer but you only want to speak to us? I don't understand.

OFFICER: *(impatiently)*

Yes. Just you. Your companions have been vouched for.

DEBS: *(outraged)*

They've been WHAT!?!

(But the Officer does not reply)

(Meanwhile, back in the holding area, Matt and Bob are still confused as to what to do. At that very moment, Emily and Kirsten appear in the doorway)

EMILY:

Oh, there you are. Are you coming?

MATT:

Are we WHAT? What are you even doing here? What's going on?

KIRSTEN: *(lowering voice)*

Emily gave you an alibi. Vouched for you. Said that you had nothing to do with any of this. Aren't you lucky, aye!?

BOB: *(shocked)*

She did what!? And they believed you?

EMILY:

Let's just say I have contacts – you're one of us, Matt – one of the library team. Have you never used your shhh-ing powers to get your own way?

BOB:

Shhh-ing power? What the heck? Matt, is she kidding?

MATT:

Errr... I'd rather not say. I took a sacred oath back at library school and, well – you know how it goes. Anyway, listen, what do you want, ladies?

EMILY:

For you to come with us. There's an old gent who's keen to talk to you.

MATT:

CB? *(she nods)* And he's KEEN to talk to us. He just seemed keen to confuse us earlier. Maybe he's had his Damascus moment of enlightenment!

EMILY:

Keen might be an exaggeration but he's making a little more sense now.

KIRSTEN:

Coffee. LOTS of coffee.

BOB:

I'm sorry, I've had quite enough of these adventures for one day. I can tell you quite definitely that I'm not leaving my wife and Alice here.

KIRSTEN:

Don't be overly dramatic. You really ought to. It won't take long.

BOB:

Well, I tell you – they won't be pleased with me. They'll lock me out of the house and only serve me burnt toast for the next six months.

EMILY:

You'll live. There is more at risk here than a few pieces of dry toast.

MATT:

Why both of us? Can't Bob stay and I'll come with you.

KIRSTEN:

Bob. Come on. You know you want to.

EMILY:

Believe me, it's for the best! Please just do as we say. Shut up and follow us!

(Matt and Bob watch as their 'saviours' head for the exit – shooting each other uncertain glances. Bob shrugs, then they follow Kirsten and Emily)

A WOMAN FOR ALL REASONS

EPISODE SIX: FORGOTTEN FRUITS...

BY NICK GOODMAN

SCENE 17. 'THE LUMINARY TAVERN'. NIGHT.

(The early hours. A lock-in at a very old pub filled with faded theatrical types. The side door opens and in steps Emily, Kirsten and then Bob and Matt; they look too anxious to be obviously tired)

EMILY: *(brightly)*

A little more relaxed than a police station, don't you think?

BOB:

What is this freak show?

EMILY:

'The Luminary Tavern'. Home to theatre folks of yore.

MATT: *(world-wearily)*

You mean washed out luvvies?

EMILY:

If you like.

BOB:

So, is CB here somewhere?

(Emily nods, slightly distractedly)

101

MATT: *(aggravated)*

Well, let's get on with it and then get back to the girls – hopefully before they notice that we're even gone.

EMILY: *(Beckoning to the man behind the bar)*

Graham, where's CB?

(Graham is 60, gay, wiry and a tad wary of questions)

GRAHAM:

And who might you be, lady?

EMILY:

A friend.

GRAHAM:

Of whom?

EMILY: *(rolling eyes)*

Of CB?   –

GRAHAM:

And he is…?

MATT: *(to Graham)*

Jake Treherne.

GRAHAM:

Well, why didn't you say?

MATT:

Well???

GRAHAM:

Oh, they stuck him in 'The Casket'.

BOB:

The WHAT!?!

GRAHAM:

The room up the stairs immediately to your left.

KIRSTEN:

Why's it called 'The Casket'?

GRAHAM:

This boozer used to be run by Jack the Ripper nuts before Timmo took over. Weirdoes. There's still some of their crap around.

(Pointing to a pitiful severed wax head on a high shelf)

That's Johnny. I wanted to throw him out, but Big Bruno fancied him so he bought the horrible thing.

MATT:

Oh… Okay. They're someone for everyone, aye? Up the stairs, you say?

(Graham nods. Bob and Matt race up to 'The Casket')

GRAHAM: *(Raising an eyebrow)*

Yes!

KIRSTEN: *(following the men)*

Let's get this over with. This place is gives me the willies.

GRAHAM: *(under his breath)*

What would you know about willies, darling?!

(Emily follows the others)

Uh-hum!

(Emily turns)

A token of appreciation would be nice.

EMILY:

Don't push it. This is an illegal lock in.

(Graham pours himself a Scotch and downs it in one)

GRAHAM:

Is there no one conscious at this hour that's any fun!!!??

('The Casket' has a playfully Gothic style. A tall, coated figure slumbers in a rocking chair in the corner. A stuffed witch's cat sits opposite. CB is sat by a fire with his feet in a tub of hot water and his neck. Matt and Bob enter and sit by CB)

CB:

Ahh, here are the heroes!

(Matt and Bob exchange bemused looks)

Good to see you again. I gather you have quite a story to tell me?

MATT:

We were hoping you could tell us.

BOB:

You weren't too keen on us being around before.

CB:

Oh that. Well, I needed the push to make the break-through.

MATT:

In that case, we're needed elsewhere.

(Matt and Bob get up, but the way is blocked by Emily and Kirsten)

EMILY:

Now boys, don't be in such a hurry. Don't we all need answers?

MATT:

Tell me why my wife and Aunt are with the cops!

KIRSTEN:

I was wondering that myself.

105

EMILY:

A charge of assault on CB.

BOB:

That's just not true.

EMILY:

When he was with you, he was conscious. Along came your family and suddenly he's not. I was only putting two and two together.

MATT:

So, you were spying on us?

KIRSTEN:

I didn't know what she was doing.

EMILY:

Your ladies will come to no harm. I need time to bring you up to speed.

KIRSTEN:

My mum must be worried sick by now!

EMILY:

Oh, do be quiet, child.

(To Matt) They were too close. They had seen too much. I want to know how much.

MATT:

The power of sshh-sh in other words.

EMILY:

I like to keep in with the local authorities. Now....

(Sitting opposite CB)

We haven't much time.

CB:

You must be Emily. The officer told me about you.

EMILY:

We have a common interest in Lady Walsh.

CB:

Her 'vibe', rather.

EMILY: *(closer)*

Is she dead or alive?

CB:

Something is alive. It came through Crystal. And it took me!

MATT:

It was as if you were channelled.

KIRSTEN:

Like a TV?

BOB:

No, he means like a ghost was communicating through him.

CB: *(nonplussed for a moment)*

No, that is nonsense. I was hypnotised!

KIRSTEN:

So, no ghost? *(to Emily)* No ghost.

EMILY:

Then where is she and what did she do to you?

CB: *(screwing his eyes up in concentration)*

I'm trying to remember. *(To Matt and Bob)* What exactly did happen?

MATT:

So, you don't remember a bloody thing!

BOB:

When you put your crystal set on, you had some kind of fit. You waffled something that sounded Celtic, burst out of the door, and fell flat on your face in the dark.

CB: *(clutching his bruised face)*

I thought someone had hit me.

(Kirsten looks accusingly at Emily who gives her best smug "Aren't I clever?" smile)

EMILY: *(softly to Kirsten)*

According to eyewitnesses, Auntie held him whilst Debs hit him.

KIRSTEN:

Mmmm, you could get done for that!!

EMILY:

Let's just say there is a mutual benefit.

SCENE 18. INT. POLICE INTERVIEW ROOM. NIGHT.

(Alice and Debs are sat in an indignant silence – understandably not at all happy – before them an embarrassed young policeman, PC Carr)

ALICE:

So apparently these days it's okay for the police to act like kidnappers. At least kidnappers tell you why they've taken you!

PC CARR:

Sorry Madam. Senior officer will be with you at any moment.

DEBS: *(to Alice)*

They even took my make-up bag.

ALICE:

Probably thought you'd hang yourself with it. According to the police you can hang yourself with just about anything!

DEBS:

Are we allowed a question? Just one thing. Why us and not the fellas?

ALICE:

He's not going to say anything, dear. He doesn't have a script! It's that Emily stirring things. I had her number when we first met her. Devious. Don't you worry, love. We have rather more questions for them than they'd like.

(Chief Superintendent Tavistock enters; a portly tired looking man in his fifties; clearly reaching out for retirement like a man searching for water in the desert. He looks distracted and as he takes his seat, he keeps looking at his watch and shuffles his papers – he looks slightly uncomfortable about being there – as if he feels that he hasn't the energy to deal with the ladies)

TAVISTOCK:

Morning ladies. I'm Chief Superintendent Tavistock. I shall be overseeing this interview.

DEBS:

Charmed, I'm sure.

(Tavistock reaches over and switches on a tape machine)

TAVISTOCK:

This interview is commencing at 3.30am.

(Debs yawns loudly)

Present is myself, Superintendent Tavistock, Alice Harrison and Debra Tully.

(Alice points to Carr, just as Tavistock addresses his next comment to him.)

That will be all officer.

(Carr leaves the room. Tavistock's manner relaxes immediately, and he switches off the tape machine. He gives the ladies his warmest smile)

Now then, a little chat off the record, I think.

(Debs opens her mouth, but Alice puts a cautionary hand on her shoulder)

ALICE:

Does that mean we are being tape recorded under the table?

TAVISTOCK:

Of course not. And do you think we have the budget for another machine when we still use tape recorders?

DEBS:

The technology is out there.

TAVISTOCK:

Yes, tell me about what you would use?

DEBS:

Never mind about that now. Why are we here?

ALICE:

Emily Bradnock. That's why. That MADAM!

TAVISTOCK:

A complaint of assault on one Jake Treherne.

DEBS: *(confused)*

I'm sorry? Who the hell is that?

TAVISTOCK:

You were with him at his railways shack this evening.

ALICE:

That was CB. We'd only just met him.

TAVISTOCK:

Somehow that makes it worse.

DEBS:

He was terrorising my husband and his friend. They had a kind of
séance apparently. We found him flaked out on the ground outside the
shack. Then he went berserk and chased us – set his dogs on us and
everything.

TAVISTOCK:

Chased you? Come on ladies, you exaggerate – my men saw no dogs.

ALICE:

Well, they wouldn't have. It was a kind of illusion. It's hard to explain!

TAVISTOCK:

Is it now? Well, I must say, this is all sounding very shaky.

ALICE:

So, when are we supposed to have battered him?

TAVISTOCK: *(checking his notes)*

Half an hour later. Apparently, you circled round the shack, entered it and, at some point around this time, you assaulted Mr Treherne.

DEBS:

How exactly are we meant to have done this or did Emily not mention that?

TAVISTOCK:

He was lying on the floor in distress at the time. And they were there. Taking pictures. It's all been documented. I can assure you of that.

ALICE: *(truth dawns)*

Ahh, I see – that explains why you took my phone. I understand now.

TAVISTOCK:

Circumstantial evidence.

ALICE: *(tightly)*

But of what?

TAVISTOCK:

Now what do you mean?

DEBS:

What is CB... err Mr Treherne doing in that shack anyway? Bit of an odd bod. Does he own it or was he trespassing too. Squatting illegally perhaps?

TAVISTOCK: *(regarding his notes as he speaks)*

113

He is known to us. Was a theatre engineer until they went computer based. He refused to work with it, and they slung him out. Went into railway communication on one of the smaller lines. He was a dead weight there too. They gave him that shack in lieu of redundancy. Still picks up work here and there as a repair man. Rather a sad old fella really, I'll admit.

ALICE:

Getting back to the point, I'd like my phone back if you don't mind. Untampered with. I depend on it on a daily basis, I'll have you know.

(The room door opens and a grim-faced PC Carr hands Tavistock a note. Tavistock opens keenly, reading it under his breath with a doomed look)

TAVISTOCK: *(to Carr)*

Nothing?

CARR: *(to Tavistock)*

Nothing.

(Tavistock resists the urge to crumple the note and instead folds it rather aggressively before sticking it absentmindedly into his top pocket)

ALICE:

If you could oblige Chief Superintendent. Please. Before I call my lawyer.

(Tavistock and Alice exchange the loaded stares of adversaries. Alice can't resist a smile as she senses that she has the upper hand)

TAVISTOCK: *(resignedly)*

Alright... Wait there.

(Tavistock leaves the room with Carr with an air of undisguised frustration. Debs turns curiously to talk to Alice who puts a finger to her lips and indicates someone or something is listening. Debs mimes the operating of a mobile phone and Morse code device. Alice mimes holding a phone, flutters her fingers from the phone to Debs, then mimes pushing a button on the mimed phone and gives a wave. Debs excitedly acknowledges then laughs)

ALICE:

You know it may be nearly four in the morning, but I doubt I'll ever sleep again. So much excitement. I must be running on sheer adrenaline.

SCENE 19. INT. 'THE LUMINARY TAVERN'. NIGHT

(All are gathered in 'The Casket', where the attention is on CB)

KIRSTEN:

What's this to do with a little old lady, for goodness sake?

CB:

I was subjected to hypnotronic influence via that old set of mine. It was an attack – maybe even a warning.

BOB:

If you say, so Professor Hawkings.

CB: *(firmly)*

I'm a scientist!

BOB:

You're a chucked-out engineer living in a railway shack and that's only because the rail yard didn't need it.

EMILY:

More importantly did Walsh – for the sake of argument – talk to you?

CB:

My mind is blank. Had a thumping headache when I woke and found these two women standing over me.

MATT:

Well, they didn't hit you that's for sure. We cut your connection.

CB:

Well yes. We've established that.

BOB:

Well, Emily has established something completely different. And it's time that we got them out of their predicament and spoke to the Police.

EMILY: *(impatiently)*

In good time. They are there to keep them out of the way. Firstly, I need you to knit together what we've discovered.

MATT: *(gesturing to CB)*

The point, dear lady, is that there is nothing to knit with. He can't remember a thing. So where do we go from here?

CB: *(ignoring Matt)*

I summoned up two ravenous dogs. What more do you want?

KIRSTEN:

Where do they fit in though? Why dogs?

CB: *(keen to be of use)*

I know that Walsh looked after dogs. She was patron of the Dog's Trust.

BOB:

So, am I right in saying that she is communicating all this via medium links?

(CB opens his mouth to speak.)

...or ultrasonics or hypnotics or whatever. Is it a fail-safe?

EMILY: *(excited)*

And the Boy Scout bit. She was a patron of them too.

KIRSTEN:

Loaded this old bird wasn't she!! It's a shame I wasn't around to benefit - what about the Girl Guides or The Brownies for that matter.

MATT:

Good point. But what exactly is Lady Walsh trying to say?

CB:

Well, those other women might know. The old girl was faffing with her phone. Not sure if she was taking a photo or what. There was a message coming through on Crystal at the time.

BOB:

Morse code. They were trying to record it.

CB:

I'll tell you one thing, I'm pretty sure that the old girl seemed to twig what was going on. She seemed to recognise something in the message.

MATT:

In short, all our answers are at the police station and not here. Emily, what are you playing at?

EMILY:

I told you what we're doing, we're keeping them out of the way so that we have a chance to collate our information.

BOB:

No, there is something else going on here.

(To CB) You've had the odd message on Crystal over the years, haven't you?

CB:

The odd random phrase. Untainted by digital snobbery.

MATT:

Like what, exactly?

CB:

Stuff about looking after things. Preserving them. Worrying about change. Institutions mostly. Charities.

EMILY:

Come on, come on lads.

(Indicating)

This is the box, think outside of it.

CB:

She mentioned Mason or Mason's. Is that a shop chain? It came up a lot. Maybe she was a shareholder or secretly owns the company.

KIRSTEN:

The Masons? Not those weirdoes who roll up their trouser legs and have funny handshakes. They give me the creeps. Like the world really needs more alpha males whispering away behind closed doors.

EMILY:

Yeah. Well, that's men for you – but we're getting off the point.

CB: *(deep in thought)*

I guess, freemasonry could be the answer.

BOB:

The Masons are usually made up of top professional people. Judges, politicians, lawyers, university professors... *(with a grin)* ...piano teachers!

CB:

Not forgetting policemen.

(Bob and Matt look at each other in alarm)

BOB:

Not forgetting policemen!!! Of course!

EMILY:

Why? What about them?

MATT: *(standing angrily over Emily)*

The power of ssshhh-ush indeed! You sold Debs and Alice out. They have found something out that the police want a lid on!!!

EMILY:

Oh, come on… like what?

BOB:

Like those sounds on Alice's phone. The Morse code. It may be something that the police want. The message. Come on, we've wasted enough time.

(Bob and Matt rush out. Before they reach the side door, Matt stops Bob)

MATT:

I wonder if they know that Alice has sent her recording to Deb's email?

BOB:

If they could just delete it from the phone. Then they'd only have

Emily's word that it was ever on there.

MATT: *(mock serious)*

You mean who don't believe in the power of ssshhh-ush?

(Bob smiles and they both leave via the side door. Back in 'The Casket', Emily stands furious over CB and Kirsten)

EMILY:

I'm surrounded by imprudent idiots!

CB:

What do you mean?

EMILY:

They will now go and spring the girls before we're ready.

KIRSTEN:

But you wanted them to 'join the dots up' didn't you?

EMILY:

Child, that was on my terms. I am the puppet mistress and my puppets have just buggered off.

KIRSTEN: *(snapping at last)*

Then bollocks to you, puppet mistress!! It's like a bad dream that won't stop. I'm off home. I've had it up to here with you. You're frigging mental the lot of you. See you Friday.

(Kirsten turns to go then spins back round, brandishing her mobile)

And if you even think of sacking me 'old girl' you might consider what

I've recorded on my phone. Neville's going to love this!!

(Kirsten flounces off. Emily turns her ire on CB)

EMILY:

And you! And a fat lot of good you were. You came highly recommended.

CB:

By the Marquis?

KIRSTEN: *(bobbing her head cheekily round the door again, smugly)*

That's the other thing. The Marquis didn't run because he was scared by a ghost. He knew the police were in on the Walsh thing and he didn't want to them looking into his muck.

EMILY:

What muck?

KIRSTEN:

Porn! He probed the police, so the police threatened to probe him. He shot porn films. Close to the knuckle stuff too.

CB:

Really?

EMILY:

How do you know all this, child?

KIRSTEN:

Because he asked me to be in one when I was at a 'Kiss' gig.

122

CB:

And did you?

(Kirsten cheekily taps her nose before flouncing off once more)

She's not as stupid as she looks, is she?

EMILY:

"Not forgetting the police" This is all your fault, you filthy freak.

CB: *(kicking his foot bowl over sending the water sizzling into the fire)*

Who the hell do you think you are??? Sending me your snooping strangers. Uninvited. I've never even met you before!!! You play your own game. I'm not helping you anymore.

EMILY: *(pointing at CB)*

You are a little man in a big, big world. I know how big. I work in a library, I know. You'll regret crossing me!

(Emily stalks off at last, slamming the door of 'The Casket' and waking the drunken figure in the rocking chair. The figure groans.)

CB:

Oh, go back to sleep, Darcy!

DARCY:

What's the noise?

CB:

A jumped-up young sleuth. Nothing else.

DARCY:

What did she want?

CB:

We were trying to track someone down.

DARCY:

Who?

CB:

We only have a surname. Walsh. She was some kind of local benefactor. We think she is hiding somewhere.

DARCY:

Walsh? Not Constance Walsh? She was a big cheese.

CB:

Could be. *(Suddenly)* Was?

DARCY:

She was the most amazing support for the local theatre.

CB:

Really? Can you introduce me?

DARCY:

Don't be absurd, old boy. She's dead.

CB:

But she can't be.

DARCY:

As the proverbial door knocker. I can show you the plaque if you like. Little one by the exit door of the Rook Theatre. Oh no, hang on. No, the bloody Tories closed it down thirty years ago. There's progress for you!

CB: *(helping Darcy to his feet)*

But is this plaque still there?

DARCY:

Yes. But the whole place is a children's play centre now. So...

CB:

SO... you'll take me there?

DARCY:

That might take some arranging in my current state. I could draw you a map!

CB: *(with force)*

Now. I'm pretty sure you can make it.

DARCY:

Be reasonable, I can barely walk and it's Lord knows when in the morning.

CB: *(CB grabs Darcy by the collar and his tone grows threatening)*

Now look, you lush, I've gone through hell because of this wretched woman, I need to know what's going on. This could be my first real evidence. Be she alive or be she dead?

DARCY:

Come on. Have pity on an old man.

CB:

I do. Me. And it means I'm one step ahead of that manipulative harpy with her two hacks. Time to go, old man. No dawdling now.

(CB trundles Darcy out of 'The Casket' and out of the side door of the Tavern. Without looking up, Graham kisses a pint glass that he is cleaning)

GRAHAM: *(to glass)*

Derry's Bubbling Brew. Helping sad losers have fun since 1982. Never fails!

A WOMAN FOR ALL REASONS

EPISODE SEVEN: INTERESTED PARTIES...

BY PAUL CHANDLER

SCENE 20. INT. A COUNTRY HOUSE, SYDNEY, AUSTRALIA, PM

(In a luxuriant country house somewhere in Australia a large middle-aged gentleman lounges on a pile of cushions upon an expensive looking bed, he is not sleeping but is reading a retro Sci-fi/Adventure comic book from the late 70s or 80s, entitled 'THE MISADVENTURES OF TWIDDLER'. He doesn't notice as his bedroom door opens and a nervous-looking young man enters)

MAN: *(keen for a response)*

Well, Hercules?

HERCULES: *(pleased to have good news)*

Your bid was successful, sir.

MAN: *(happy, but quietly so)*

Marvellous! How much did it cost me?

HERCULES:

Significantly less than you were expecting?

MAN:

For the whole run?

127

HERCULES:

For the whole run, sir – yes... A snip at seven thousand five hundred.

MAN:

My goodness! That was a bargain. Well done, you've done me proud.

HERCULES:

For one hundred and twenty-five issues, yes... Most certainly.

MAN: *(concerned)*

One hundred and twenty-six is the full set – there was a summer special remember? I do hope it's one hundred and twenty-six, Hercules. Don't let one copy be missing. That really would spoil the value.

HERCULES: *(apologetic)*

I'm sorry, sir. Sorry. Yes... You're right. One hundred and twenty-six. That is what I meant. My apologies.

MAN: *(reassuringly)*

Good. We will count them together when they arrive.

(Before Hercules can reply, the bedroom door opens, and an elderly woman enters. She shoots Hercules a knowing look and he quickly makes his exit)

WOMAN: *(disapprovingly)*

What have you been wasting your money on now, Edmund? Not more comics? Oh, I despair.

MAN/EDMUND: *(gritting his teeth and remaining polite)*

Please don't! But yes, Mother – comics – exactly that. I am now the proud owner of a complete run of '*THE MISADVENTURES OF*

TWIDDLER...!'

MOTHER: *(attempting to show interest)*

Is that one you used to write for or one you used to collect as a boy?

EDMUND: *(calmly, close to patronising)*

One I used to collect, Mother.

MOTHER:

I always told you that you should have looked after them better.

EDMUND:

If I remember clearly, I think you used to tell me off for keeping them at all. I came home from university one holiday only to find them smouldering on a bonfire in the back garden; that really was a fine welcome home.

MOTHER:

It was cold, we needed fuel for the fire.

EDMUND:

Nonsense! It was July, Mother. Still, that was a very long time ago now.

MOTHER: *(playfully)*

It was indeed. Have you ever forgiven me?

EDMUND: *(bluntly)*

The jury is out.

MOTHER: *(chuckling almost unkindly)*

Much as I expected. I don't know. I thought you'd grow out of them –

129

but you never did. They're the love of your life, aren't they?

EDMUND:

Maybe…

MOTHER:

But they are, dear. You and your superhero magazines. Inseparable!

EDMUND: *(put out)*

Twiddler was not a superhero. If anything, he was an anti-hero – a villain. Although whether he considered himself as such I very much doubt...

MOTHER:

Criminals never do dear. Look at the world's politicians. Or maybe don't!

EDMUND:

Hmm. You probably don't realise quite how ground-breaking Twiddler was, mother. It was unusual to have an anti-hero leading the action.

MOTHER:

I guess you're right. Maybe in the world of comics – having a baddie as the leading man; it must have raised a few eyebrows, I suspect. Although - of course – in the world of literature, Raffles was also along similar lines.

EDMUND:

Twiddler is nothing like Raffles, mother. Not even slightly.

MOTHER: *(wistfully)*

Oh. What a shame. I did love Raffles. So charming! I always wanted to be whisked away by him or someone like him. But no... I had to stay here.

EDMUND:

The antics of Twiddler should hardly be new to you, Mother. I'm pretty sure I talked about nothing else when I was in my mid-teens.

MOTHER:

You could be right, dear. I forget now.

EDMUND:

Did you want something, Mother? I'm actually rather busy!

MOTHER: *(deliberately trying to annoy)*

What? Lounging around in here? Shouldn't you be working, dear?

EDMUND: *(insistently)*

Lounging – as you so incorrectly refer to it – is my work.

MOTHER:

Really? How odd.

EDMUND:

If you simply must know absolutely everything about my day – I am waiting for a phone call.

MOTHER: *(curious)*

Oooh! Really? How exciting...

EDMUND:

You make receiving a phone call sound like something unusual.

MOTHER:

Well dear, when it's you then it usually is exciting news, one way or another!

EDMUND:

Flatter me all you like, Mother – but I'm still not going to tell you anymore.

(Mother looks frustrated, but before she can say anything further the phone begins to ring and Edmund puts down his magazine, making shooing movements to indicate that she should leave, which – very grudgingly - she does, although she pauses in the hall hoping to hear some of his conversation. Expecting this, Edmund puts his call on hold, gets up and goes to the bedroom door, making it clear to his mother that she has been seen. Having done so he closes the door firmly and returns to the phone)

I'm sorry. I was being overheard... Mother. She's gone now. So, tell me, is everything in place? It is? Good! Yes, I saw your email. Most interesting. Well... Thank you for letting me know. I presume that you'll be back in touch when you have more information for me. Marvellous. Alright then, I'll speak to you again soon.

(Edmund looks very pleased with himself as he breaks the call. He fumbles with his phone and brings up his emails He is looking at some small thumb- nail photos. The faces are familiar: Matt, Bob, Debs, Alice, Emily, Kirsten.)

SCENE 21. INT. MAJORCA, A HOLIDAY APARTMENT, NIGHT

(A sunny location, a spotlessly clean apartment with minimal 'modern' decoration. A couple in their mid-30s sit, deep in conversation. They are dressed in a casual yet fashionable style. There is a baby-monitor on the table. As they speak, they appear distracted by one of their staff who is busy attempting to clean this room and another that is attached to it)

MAN: *(excitedly)*

I really can't wait for tonight's episode. It'll be a good one, I think. It just seems to get better every week. It's quite astonishing, really…

WOMAN: *(in agreement)*

Oh, I do hope so. Last week's cliff-hanger was wonderful, I thought.

MAN:

I don't know where they get their ideas.

WOMAN:

Darling, you do know that it's not scripted!

(The Man looks blankly at her)

Are you being funny? You DO know it's not scripted? Right? RIGHT!?

MAN: *(unsure)*

I'm sorry? I'm not sure what you mean.

WOMAN: *(almost laughing)*

Seriously? You must do? You must know that it's all real – it's far more like reality television than an actual drama with a script involved.

MAN: *(completely surprised)*

Really? You're kidding. Oh, I completely hate reality TV. It's a scourge on modern society. At least that's what I read on Twitter.

WOMAN:

Oh, you are funny. What on earth is the difference?

MAN:

I don't understand.

WOMAN: *(almost mocking)*

Well, what's the difference between watching a drama – or watching reality TV? The drama is full of odd characters doing odd things – just like the reality show. The only difference is that one is real, and one isn't.

MAN: *(stupidly stubborn)*

Don't be ridiculous; it's completely different and you know it.

WOMAN:

Why? Because you feel happier in knowing that the people doing the things may be unpleasant – but at least they're not real. Is that it?

MAN:

Nonsense. Listen, I have things to do. Enjoy your reality TV.

(The woman laughs as the man strides silently from the room, but then seems slightly upset when she realises that her companion is genuinely cross with her. She shrugs – and then notices that one of her staff is nervously standing in the doorway wondering if it is okay to continue cleaning.)

WOMAN: *(calmly/kindly)*

Georgio. Come in. It's fine to clean in here.

GEORGIO: *(worried/nervous)*

I'm sorry, Madame. I wasn't sure. Your husband... He was cross.

WOMAN:

It's okay, come in! We were having disagreements over TV programmes. Well, I'm not even sure it counts as a TV show if you watch on the internet.

GEORGIO:

Do you mean like Youtube? Or different.

WOMAN: *(eyeing him with a smile, almost teasing)*

Different. It's an actual dedicated channel. Well, anyway... It doesn't matter! I don't suppose you have time for TV. When you're young you don't want to be indoors. You want to be out enjoying yourself. Am I right?

GEORGIO:

Well, yes. I suppose. But there is always time.

WOMAN:

Well, let me show you. It might amuse you. No, leave your work for the moment. Come in. Close the door. If you would like to see, I mean…

GEORGIO: *(politely)*

Yes, Madame. I am interested. Thank you for this experience.

WOMAN:

Then come here. Sit by me.

(Georgio gingerly crosses the room to the sofa where the woman is lounging.)

(Quickly she grabs the young man's hand – taking control as she pushes him down on the bed – kissing him passionately, hungrily. Georgio responds excitedly and the two of them begin to undress – lost in their

135

passion. Suddenly we are watching the seduction through a monitor screen – the scene expands until we see that other members of staff are watching events down in the kitchen. The cook tuts and shakes her head – she shoos the other staff back to their jobs and then presses a button by the screen – the scene changes and we begin to see familiar faces from our own story – including the events from the following scene (22) from back in the UK)

Meanwhile, back at the Police Station...

SCENE 22. INT. THE POLICE STATION, NIGHT

(Alice and Debs are still in The Police Station, although they are no longer being questioned – they are merely waiting to have their belongings returned so that they can leave, but there is a delay)

DEBS: *(with simmering fury)*

What on earth is going on here? How long can it take to get our stuff back for goodness sakes?

ALICE:

I've a theory, but I am loath to discuss it whilst we remain in this building.

DEBS:

Oh, yes? Then wait and tell me when we leave.

ALICE: *(blithely)*

That's if we leave before that 'lovely' Mr Trump gets frustrated and accidentally presses the big red button.

DEBS:

I do hope you're being sarcastic, Auntie?

ALICE:

About him pressing the big red button?

DEBS:

No. That's almost inevitable. No, about him being lovely!

ALICE:

Of course, I was definitely being sarcastic about that bit.

DEBS:

Oh! Thank goodness for that. I thought you'd come over all funny.

ALICE: *(affectionately)*

How EVER could you have thought that I genuinely meant it; daft apeth.

DEBS: *(grinning, but distracted)*

Alright. Okay, I'm stupid. I wasn't concentrating. Listen, should I go and speak to someone? At very least if we're not being held for questioning, I think we definitely deserve a cup of coffee or something.

ALICE:

Well, it's early, dear. There aren't a lot of staff on duty.

DEBS:

All the more reason to let us go. You don't think they're waiting until daylight or something. Because they're worried about us being on the streets so early in the morning?

137

ALICE:

Because they think we might cause a disturbance?

DEBS:

No, silly. Because they think it's dangerous for us.

ALICE:

If they thought it was dangerous, they could have driven us home about an hour ago. It's almost 6am, do you realise that?

DEBS:

Yes. We've been here for absolutely hours

And for WHAT?!

ALICE:

Well, as I say, I have my theories. *(Lowers her voice)* I think it's a delaying tactic – they've questioned us, but know we've done nothing wrong. Now they're resorted to pretending they've misplaced my handbag and your coat.

DEBS:

For what reason, exactly?

ALICE:

To give the others a head start.

DEBS:

To do WHAT?

ALICE:

Well, it's a possibility, isn't it? Don't you think?

DEBS: *(surprised)*

But why would they want the others to get a head start? Are you saying that the Police are in on this or something?

ALICE: *(thinking it through)*

In on what though? I must say I have no idea of how any of this fits together – at least not at the moment.

DEBS: (confidently)

It's okay. We'll work it out.

(These scenes are being watched through one-way glass by Carr and Tavistock.)

CARR: (irritated)

They're whispering? I can't hear what they're saying?

TAVISTOCK: *(patiently)*

Of course, they're whispering, Carr – they know something is up – they know we're keeping them here for as long as possible, just because.

CARR: *(with uncertainty)*

So, we don't mind that they're whispering?

TAVISTOCK:

Not really! Give them another 10 minutes and then send them on their way. I'm just waiting for the okay! You do have their belongings ready, I hope.

CARR:

Errr... Yeah... Somewhere... No... No.. Really... I know where it all is.

TAVISTOCK: *(slowly, carefully)*

Good. Well, run along then and prepare to show our guests the door.

CARR:

Are you saying that in a deliberately sinister way or is that just how you speak?

TAVISTOCK:

It's just how I speak, thank you very much.

(Just then Tavistock is distracted by an alert on his computer screen, it reads: 'LET THEM GO – WE WANT TO SEE WHAT HAPPENS NEXT.. ')

TAVISTOCK: *(determinedly)*

Okay! The time is right; show them out! Give them my apologies, won't you?

CARR:

Oh... Sure... Yes, alright... I'll do that.

(Tavistock mumbles something and, once Carr has left the room, he flicks the channel on his monitor screen, and we see Carr approaching the ladies. We do not hear them speak but watch as their belongings are returned to them. Alice and Debs hurriedly head off on their way)

ALERT! PROGRESSING TO NEXT STAGE...

(Reads the words on the screen. It is at this point that we begin to realise that Tavistock is not the only one watching – we see many screens and many faces watching – all eager to view what might occur next...

A WOMAN FOR ALL REASONS

EPISODE EIGHT: I HEARD A RUMOUR...

BY NICK GOODMAN

SCENE 23. DEB'S LIVING ROOM, DAY

(It is morning at long last. Deb is slumped in a chair asleep, so tired she never made it to bed. Alice enters in a dressing gown, fresh as a posy and holding a cup of tea, which she offers to Deb. Gently she shakes her niece awake with her free hand, careful not to spill any of the drink)

ALICE:

Wakey, wakey, sleepy bunny. I've brought you a cuppa. From the looks of it you could probably do with something a little stronger, however...

DEB: *(Stirring, stretching, still a little disorientated)*

Tea will do me just fine to start with! Oh wow. What time is it?

ALICE:

Seven o'clock.

DEB:

Oh Auntie, I've only been asleep for two hours! I need at least six – and eight is my norm. I'm going to be a complete zombie at this rate.

ALICE:

Come on... No excuses. We've work to do.

DEB:

Oh dear, have we? I just don't think I'm going to be good for anything in my current state but I can see you won't take no for an answer. How

142

are you able to look so perky, Auntie? You're unbelievable.

ALICE:

My grey matter has been buzzing after last night.

DEB: *(hugging a pillow)*

It's like a bad dream We should never have got involved!

ALICE:

There are still questions to be answered. Where do you keep your laptop?

DEB: *(without looking up)*

Oh, is that all, I could have told you that any time. It's in the cupboard by the telly. What are you doing?

ALICE:

That message. We must decode it. I have the oddest feeling if the police haven't finished with us, neither have other people.

(Matt enters in a dressing gown, half asleep)

DEB:

Oh Matt, be a love and make us some breakfast. Bacon and eggs? Oh, and some buttered toast… Coffee… You'll find all you need in the fridge.

MATT:

Err… Right! Yes, me lady!

(Matt walks sleepily back out to the kitchen. He and Bob pass, barely aware of each other. Bob also appears zonked)

ALICE: *(reaching into the cupboard and pulling out the laptop)*

Bob, spare room. Deb still has a 'Girl Guide' book I gave her.

(Looking at Deb)

At least I think you have. You didn't throw it out, did you?

(Debs nods to confirm it should still be there and raises two thumbs)

Please – be a dear, Bob – go and fetch it for me, will you?

BOB:

Whatever for?

ALICE: *(sitting at the table and switching on the laptop)*

You'll see.

(Bob stumbles off)

DEB:

"Whatever for?" would be my question too!

ALICE: *(impatiently, signing in)*

Morse code. It's from the same time as our friend Lady Walsh. I'm sure all these things are on the internet somewhere, but I prefer a paper source.

DEB: *(moving closer)*

Okay... So, Auntie... This Walsh woman. Did you know her?

ALICE: *(distractedly)*

Mmm?

DEB:

Auntie, you seem to be throwing yourself into this mystery. Remember when you talked to that crystal set that sent CB curly-wurly...

ALICE:

Yes, dear – of course I do – it was only last night. Why?

DEB:

Well, you seemed to know who you were talking to.

ALICE: *(feigning innocence)*

Did I? Really… How strange.

(Alice turns back to the computer as she logs on…)

Well, I'm like that. I'm well-disposed to people. Even the great disembodied.

(Bob enters with a moth-eaten Girl Guiding book and places it on the table.)

BOB:

There it is. I don't know why, but there it is.

ALICE:

Splendid. It's for Morse Code.

BOB:

But are you sure it actually was Morse?

ALICE: *(holding up fingers in the Girl Guide salute)*

What do you think?

DEB:

Is the internet on, love?

BOB:

It's never off, you make sure of that.

DEB:

Good isn't it? That Auntie and I are helping you with your mystery.

BOB:

Actually Deb, to tell you the truth.

ALICE:

Yes.

BOB:

Nothing. I'll just check Facebook on my phone.

DEB:

Matt is making us all a spot of breakfast. *(Stretching)* Can we put the news on, Auntie – or will it distract you too much?

ALICE: *(staring hard at the laptop screen)*

It will, I'm afraid. At least for now – I really need absolute quiet to concentrate. Now, with luck, my email will have come through.

BOB: *(looking up)*

Email?

DEB:

Yes. I did tell you last night. Before we were herded away. Auntie emailed herself the sound file to her Google account then deleted the original.

BOB:

Ah, we hoped you'd do something like that.

ALICE:

Then we must also delete this version after we've decoded it.

BOB:

Because of the police?

ALICE:

I think they will be licking their wounds after last night. Contrary to popular belief, they do need a valid reason to actually burst in.

BOB:

So, we're safe?

ALICE:

No one is safe online anymore. Security, Malware, the whole boiling lot. I get the distinct impression that there is someone very clever on our trail.

DEB: *(curious)*

Who exactly?

ALICE:

Well, I wouldn't trust that Madam, Emily. Bit too sharp for her own good that one. I'd really like to know what she's up to.

BOB:

We're way ahead of her, that's for sure.

DEB:

I wonder. Maybe Matt knows something more about her.

ALICE: *(reaching her emails and opening them)*

Maybe… We must ask him later… Ah! Here we are…

(Clicking the vital email)

Sound file. Yes! It's okay. Good. Now Deb, I need something to write with.

BOB: *(Passing Alice a pen)*

Allow me!

(Alice takes the pen and clicks it into action)

ALICE:

Right, total silence whilst I listen

(The audio file sounds out. There is a crackle and oscillation, and the sound of a Morse beat can be heard. Alice scribbles down what she hears, referencing the book. There is a notification sound alert from Bob's phone. Alice hisses as she writes. A few seconds later, Matt drops something hot in the kitchen and expletives can be heard. Alice mutters "Silence" under her breath. The message continues for several minutes. Then it stops. Alice scans through what she has read and double checks with her Guidebook.)

BOB: *(to Deb)*

Can we talk yet?

ALICE: *(absorbed by her work)*

No, I'll say when!

(Deb and Bob exchange "That told us "looks and Alice studies what she has put down. More mobile notification alerts sound out)

Bob, please! Can't you shut that thing off...?

BOB:

Sorry! The world and his wife seem to have sent me a message in the last few minutes. I'll put it on silent.

(Matt enters with the first couple of plates of cooked breakfast)

MATT:

Come and get it!

(Everyone shushes Matt, who shrugs and put the plates on the table)

Well, I'm starting. The bottle of ketchup is on the worktop...

(Bob and Deb move to the table and start to eat, all the time watching Alice. She eventually turns, her face creased in thought)

ALICE:

Okay, it goes something like this... "Why else would I be doing this. I am the life blood and the pulse. I need you. Lots of eyes but not many hearts. Everyone wants but not many give. I am reaching. The way is fuzzy. Who is that man? What does he want? Lead. Follow. There is a world to hold together. Above all, avoid!" Hmm... What do you make of all that, folks?

(There is a stunned silence)

DEB:

I'm not sure. But what do they mean? Avoid what?

ALICE:

I'm not sure. That was when Madam arrived with the police. *(There are more thoughtful expressions from around the room)* Well, leave some brekkers for me.

(Alice joins them at the table. A curious Bob checks Facebook on his phone.)

DEB:

Bob! Manners! Can't you just eat!

BOB:

Sorry I just want to see who needs me so badly *(Checking)* Friend request! Dozens of them! Who are these people? Never heard of them. There aren't even any mutual friends. Do I even know a Georgio? This is crazy!

(Debs and Alice crowd around Bob, curious to see what he sees. Matt just sighs – he is far more interested in the breakfast that he just took. Seeing as nobody else seems interested in their food Matt quickly steals one of Bob's bacon rashers, hiding it in a folded slice of wholemeal bread before sticking into his greedy mouth.)

SCENE 24. REFERENCE LIBRARY, DAY

(Back to the library. Emily is sat at her desk, glaring at her computer, she appears very tired and very fed up. She mutters to herself and hops between Google and social media. Neville, head librarian, pops his head around his office door. He is a non-descript, worried looking man

in his early fifties)

NEVILLE:

Emily, you're not using Facebook again. I want that cataloguing finished today. You've had three weeks – I swear that pile hasn't shrunk at all.

EMILY: *(without looking up)*

That's why Kirsten was seconded to us.

NEVILLE: *(closing his eyes)*

Not quite.

EMILY:

Well, why else is she with us?

NEVILLE: *(tightly)*

She is supposed to be doing all the tasks that haven't been attended to since since you've been promoted!

EMILY: *(a little too hotly and a little too loudly)*

Look, this is important. There is something I'm missing!

NEVILLE: *(raising an eyebrow)*

Research?

EMILY:

Yes, if you like!

Many of the silent readers shush Emily. But one or two remain staring at her, a look of curious recognition coming over them.

NEVILLE:

Oh well… *(rhetorically)* I suppose I'll just leave you to it, shall I?

(Neville disappears into his office. Emily looks at two simultaneously displayed screens, one to the other in mounting bafflement, alarm, and frustration. She fails to notice a figure enter the library: shades, raincoat, trilby, trying and failing to look inconspicuous. The figure moves stealthily around the wall of the room until they reach Emily's desk. They then duck down under it and shuffle towards her. Only then does she notice them)

EMILY:

Can I help you?

(The figure hurriedly removes their sunglasses. He is an arrogant looking, finely boned man in his mid-20s. Emily recognises him instantly and quickly mellows into a smug smile)

MAN: *(harsh whisper)*

It's ME!!

EMILY:

Well, well, well! You've got interested in reading again have you?

MAN:

You've got to help me!

EMILY:

You ran away remember. Not up to it. It was all too freaky for you.

152

MAN:

This is different. My whole world has gone mad!

EMILY:

Go and read something. I'm just not interested!

MAN:

I've had death threats!!

EMILY: *(interested, despite herself)*

Really? Why?

MAN:

People know I'm involved. Or was involved. They know everything about me and it's becoming unmanageable! I need a way out.

EMILY:

What on earth are you babbling about?

MAN:

Death threats from the parents of girls that I've worked with.

(Emily ducks under the desk and the two confront face to face on haunches, continuing their conversation in arch whispers)

EMILY:

Girls? Oh, you mean your filmic exploits. I know about that.

MAN:

How for Pete's sake?

EMILY:

Too freaky was it? In too deep? I don't think so. The police had you by the balls over your films. That's why you got out.

MAN:

But how did you find out about that?

EMILY:

Kirsten told me.

MAN:

And who is Kirsten?

EMILY:

Well, if you take so little interest in your groomed stars, it's little wonder their parents aren't happy!

MAN:

What does she look like?

EMILY:

Shortish, spiky hair, 70s-style Kiss T shirt. You know, back when they were originally in make-up. She's obsessed with them – knows the albums too – unlike some young'uns who only wear those clothes to look cool.

MAN:

Oh yes. I remember her now… Right snotty cow, I thought. Quite the attitude… Mind you, get that T-shirt off and…

EMILY: *(Emily slaps the man)*

Far too much data. What are you doing here?

MAN:

How did all this get out? I didn't say anything. Did you? What did Kirsten do, go to the paper???

EMILY:

Don't be a fool. She only told me to score a point off me. She's like that. She certainly wasn't proud of it.

MAN:

Oh... so what's going on? People seem to know about the films. The wrong kind of people. They know I was involved in the Walsh hunt. What happened?

EMILY: *(letting go the smug for a moment)*

I don't know. I've had a stream of messages about it too. A select number of people seem to know all about us.

MAN:

Oh hell, what am I going to do? I'm the Marquis of Hamilton. I can't have death threats!

EMILY:

Pull yourself together, man!

MARQUIS:

What's happened to us?

EMILY:

Somehow we seem to have become online stars. *(Moving closer)* Our lives are known. Someone is watching us.

MARQUIS:

Has anyone ever told you, you have the loveliest complexion.

(Emily slaps the Marquis and holds him by the chin like a Victorian urchin)

EMILY:

You can leave that at the door. Now listen, I can get you out of this. It's lucky for you I need friends right now.

MARQUIS:

But you got me into this!

EMILY:

The death threats would have happened anyway. You're randy and careless. You thought with your knob and now someone has got hold of it. You are going to do as I say. Man up! You are going to sell your soul to me.

MARQUIS:

I'm surprised you haven't got someone else helping you.

EMILY:

There were two of them. They were coming along nicely. Then a wife got involved. Worst still an aunt got involved!

MARQUIS:

Never a good idea.

EMILY:

They cocked everything up and got away with information that I needed.

MARQUIS:

What do you want? To get it back? *(Emily nods ruefully)* Just like that?

EMILY:

Just like that, your Grace. You've got my number?

MARQUIS:

Of course (Checking a pocket diary) Ah no.

(Emily scribbles a number on a Post-It and places it upon his forehead)

EMILY: *(grinning)*

I'm disappointed, your Grace. You've got to learn to treat women with respect. Starting with Lady Walsh. Now go to it.

(The Marquis goes to leave then Emily pulls him back)

We can turn this round very nicely. Give the public what they want.

MARQUIS: *(Head in hands)*

Please don't say that word… "public".

(The Marquis withdraws, hastily replaces his shades, and makes quickly for the door. Emily also rises from under the desk; relaxing. She faces a middle- aged woman at the desk who has been waiting for ages for attention)

157

EMILY:

Yes, can I help you?

WOMAN:

I'm trying to return this book, but the check-in doesn't work.

EMILY:

What makes you say that?

WOMAN:

There was no bleep when I put the book under the scanner.

EMILY:

Oh, you've brought it back haven't you? Just go "Bleep".

(The woman looks nonplussed. Emily bursts out laughing, enthused by her change of fortune, and delighted by her customers confused expression. At first she speaks to herself, but then raises her voice to the room in general)

Can you believe him? What is he going to do? That was the Marquis of Hamilton, you know.

(To the wider room)

And I know YOU know!

(To the woman)

BLEEP!?

WOMAN: *(utterly bewildered)*

Bleep…

SCENE 25. PLAY-ALL-DAY NURSERY. DAY

(The once proud Rook Theatre is now a day centre for pre-school children. Its doors are open and children with their parents are walking in. Its Victorian architecture now looks bizarre with a brightly coloured and sterile interior environment. Just outside the front door is a large oak tree. A bedraggled CB and Darcy lie asleep underneath it. As they pass, some of the parents look on in distain, some with amusement. CB's slumped form is gently nudged by a tiny hand. CB stirs and wakes. Standing over him is Chloe, a happy looking four-year-old girl. Standing behind her is Miss Jameson, a perky nursery teacher, who hands Chloe a bowl of hot porridge.)

MISS JAMESON: *(to Chloe)*

Go on, Chloe – don't be shy.

CHLOE: *(to CB)*

Good morning. Would you like some breakfast?

(CB groggily raises himself on one arm, blearily taking in his observers)

CB:

Breakfast? Oh, err yes. Thank you.

(CB takes the bowl)

Who are you then?

CHLOE: *(after a few shy seconds)*

Chloe.

MISS JAMESON: *(to CB)*

That's confidential. You don't need to know that.

CB: *(to Miss Jameson)*

Don't I?

(To Chloe)

To hell with conversation then, eh Chloe. Who needs it!? Not to
mention "Don't talk to strangers!"

(CB pokes Darcy awake – to Darcy)

Oi! Come on you, we're being fed!

(Darcy wakes with even more disorientation)

MISS JAMESON: *(to CB)*

Enjoy your nutritious meal, sir. After you've finished, just pop in, I have
a few forms that I need you to complete.

*(Miss Jameson ushers a giggling Chloe away and they head indoors.
CB digs into his porridge, stirring it slowly while Darcy levers himself
up.)*

DARCY:

What happened?

CB:

You already told me. The Tories closed it down.

DARCY:

No, I mean last night?

CB:

I think we had a noglet too much under this tree in the wee small hours.

DARCY:

How undignified!

CB:

Never mind, they fed us. That was Chloe, you know. Not sure about the other miss.

DARCY: *(sniffing uncertainly)*

What is it? In this bowl, I mean…

CB:

Porridge…

DARCY:

Revolting!

CB:

You're so ungrateful. Too damn working class for you. And I thought actors worried where the next meal was coming from!

DARCY:

Lidls I expect. Why feed us brekkers anyway? It's not a hotel now, is it?

CB: *(Scoffing porridge)*

It's been colonised by do-gooders.

(CB finishes his porridge and places the spoon in the empty bowl)

But never mind about that. We have a job to do.

DARCY:

What?

CB:

That plaque, man. You said it was in this building.

(Pointing at the nursery)

DARCY:

Well, I suppose it still is. But won't it look dodgy if we just waltzed in?

CB: *(Getting to his feet, dusting himself off)*

Ah no, 'Miss' has invited us in. Something about forms to fill in. I'm not really sure what she's on about – but at least it gives us a genuine alibi.

DARCY:

What? For entering the building? I guess so. Probably some security crap.

CB:

Signing off for two bowls of porridge, maybe. Well, that's our ticket in.

(Helping Darcy up, CB makes for the main entrance. Darcy follows behind. They wade through arriving children. A slight bend past the reception area brings them to the old ticket office; only its Victorian facia remains. Inside the office are dozens of coloured inflatable balls. Darcy reacts in shock)

DARCY:

That's sacrilege!!

CB:

Helium more like.

DARCY:

Poor Jack would turn in his grave.

CB:

He certainly wouldn't be able to sit anywhere. Now where's the plaque?

DARCY:

Every season we would come up to Jack at this desk and ask him, "What's on this season. What should we go for?"

CB:

So?

DARCY:

If we liked it, then we would kiss the nearest performer. It was all rather good fun.

CB:

I guess so, but I imagine Jack remained firmly behind the glass.

DARCY:

He never left his station. We were really quite choosey. If we didn't like what was on offer, we turned and spat behind us. Call it a kind of actor's ritual, if you like. Anyway, the plaque went exactly in the spot where we spat!

CB:

Quite charming. So that means it's behind us, right?

(They turn. Behind them, at knee height, is the plaque. It is currently obscured by a male toddler who is chatting animatedly to some unseen, possibly invisible companion. The language that he uses is also unknown)

Hmm… I didn't expect a queue.

(Miss Jameson trots towards them. She carries a clipboard in her hand)

MISS JAMESON:

Coooee! I've got the forms…

CB: *(Taking the clipboard and studying the forms attached to it)*

Oh good. Tell me *(Pointing to the boy)* Can anyone join in this chit-chat?

MISS JAMESON:

That's Christopher and his imaginary friend. They seem to like that corner.

DARCY:

Christopher or his friend? You encourage imaginary friends?

MISS JAMESON:

Oh yes. It increases their social skills. It's fascinating really quite how much has been written on the subject. Who knows what it all means…

CB: *(reading the forms)*

Hmm… Nothing surprises me these days. Tell me, do imaginary friends have to be safeguard checked these days?

MISS JAMESON:

There's no need to be facetious!

CB:

You may laugh *(Pausing to look at a not-laughing Miss Jameson)* ...but give it time! *(Looking closer at the form)* Look, I'm not sure that some of this is strictly accurate. It says here that we are persons of no fixed abode!

MISS JAMESON:

Yes!

DARCY:

Homeless?!

MISS JAMESON:

Yes!?

CB: *(with disgusted resignation)*

Oh well, we might as well be, the pair of us. What is this by the way?

MISS JAMESON: *(proudly)*

It's part of Chloe's Citizenship Merit Profile.

CB:

For the love of Gertrude! That Chloe – she can't be a year older than four from what I saw. Does she understand a word of this profile thing?

MISS JAMESON:

That's not really the point is it?

(A gushing young mother suddenly comes up to CB)

MUM:

I thought you were wonderful last night. You were so dominant in the pub. Can't wait to see what happens next!

(Darcy and Miss Jameson look on amazed. The mum dances away down the corridor, chatting excitedly to her child)

DARCY:

Well, you're a dark horse. You were wonderful last night, were you?

CB:

I was not! I was humiliated, dirtied and with my feet in a bucket. You were there! I've never seen that woman before in my life!

(Miss Jameson takes the completed form on its clipboard back once more from CB, looking unsure of herself)

MISS JAMESON:

Well, I mustn't detain you.

(Miss Jameson taps Christopher on the shoulder and ushers him away)

Come along Christopher, you'll see Lady Walsh at break time.

(Christopher waves to his invisible friend and allows himself to be led away down the corridor with Miss Jameson. CB and Darcy exchange "Oooh that was a clue" looks then dash for the vacated corner. CB takes out an eye glass and examines the plaque)

CB: *(reading)*

"Constance Louisa Patience Walsh. Patron and mother to the Arts, owner of the Rook Theatre."

(To Darcy) She owned you, Darcy!

(Back to plaque)

"Your legacy feeds the soul and cheers the intellect!" Bit florid isn't it?

(Swinging round on Darcy…)

Dates! There are no bloody dates. You've wasted my time!

DARCY: *(Marching up to the plaque and examining it)*

Now wait a minute… *(pausing)* I thought so! This is new!

CB:

What do you mean? It's been changed? How is it different?

DARCY:

Look at it! I'd say this was no more than ten years old. The original one would be much older.

CB:

So, the other one was scrapped?

DARCY:

Don't look at me. I've not seen this gaff since the 80s. It wouldn't surprise me if somebody sold the original on eBay and replaced it with this one.

CB: *(getting up in haste)*

Let's get out of here. We have some council heads to knock together.

(As the two turn, they face Kirsten, looking astonished at them. She does not appear to be the bored, despondent, or aggressive Kirsten as she was before. She is serious and self-conscious. At her heels is a boy

167

toddler)

KIRSTEN:

Oh, it's you. Hello!

CB:

Young Kirsten. What brings you here?

KIRSTEN: *(looking down at the boy)*

Well…I have a two-year-old. Emily doesn't know. She'd get funny with me. You don't know her. She'd be a cow about it.

DARCY:

Our lips are sealed, young lady.

KIRSTEN:

Promise you won't tell? What brings you here?

CB: *(pointing to the wall)*

The plaque down there. It's that Walsh woman. I thought it might give us a clue to where she is or who she is.

DARCY:

Or even IF she is!

KIRSTEN: *(suddenly frightened)*

You don't know do you? You don't know what's happened?

(Two more mums pass by, staring at Kirsten, noticing her as if for the first time. They go saucer eyed with recognition. Kirsten flinches)

CB:

What's wrong?

KIRSTEN:

We're being watched! Somehow. By the public. On the internet, I think.
It's gone viral! WE HAVE GONE VIRAL!
(Picking up her boy)
I wanted Lewis kept out of this. You're brought them here, haven't
you!! Just go now, please just go!!!

*(Kirsten hurries down the corridor with Lewis in her arms, upset. CB
and Darcy look gravely at each other, but then they follow her)*

A WOMAN FOR ALL REASONS

EPISODE NINE: SPIN ME ROUND...

BY PAUL CHANDLER

SCENE 26. BOB'S LIVING ROOM, LATE MORNING

(Back at Bob and Deb's house, Matt is sitting quietly in the living room, deep in thought. He holds an old school notepad and a biro and keeps scribbling things down every minute or two. Occasionally he glances out the window and down towards the back garden. It is incredibly quiet in the house, and one might almost think that he was alone. However, at exactly this moment in walks Bob, curious as to what his friend is up to)

BOB: *(somewhat confused)*

Where's everybody gone? I know idea what's going on around here today!

MATT: *(unsure)*

Oh, I dunno. I really don't. To be honest I should probably go back to my flat and do some washing. Not to mention catching up with all my backlog of 80s Top Of The Pops episodes; my Digi-box will be over-flowing!

BOB:

Priorities! Priorities! What about your work? Are you meant to be going in?

MATT: *(not sounding at all guilty)*

I'm on leave. It was all a bit short notice, but they were fine about it. They're always on at me to take it or I'll lose it.

BOB:

Same here. Well, in that case there's no need for you to rush off then. Hmm, I wonder where Debs is?

MATT:

Did you try calling her!?

BOB: *(distracted, slightly ratty, then mellowing)*

I did! No reply, of course! I suspect that the ladies have their own mission.

MATT: *(sounding a little cynical)*

Well, yeah – except their mission originally started out as our mission. But now they seem to have taken it up as their own.

BOB: *(curious for his opinion)*

They do, rather. But they're not discussing it with us. So, what next?

MATT: *(chuckling)*

It's war!

BOB: *(unsure)*

Really?!

MATT: *(boldly, but with humour)*

Of course. If they want to keep secrets, then let them keep secrets. We'll just do our own thing and follow up on our own leads.

BOB:

Make a competition of it, you mean?

MATT:

Maybe. I suppose so, yeah.

BOB:

Hmm, I'm just worried that things have already got pretty heavy. This isn't a game. You must realise that after what's happened so far. What if the ladies get themselves into trouble?

MATT: *(interjecting)*

What if WE get ourselves into trouble for that matter.

BOB: *(nodding in agreement)*

Which is probably more likely.

MATT: *(resignedly)*

Well, they don't seem to care much about that.

BOB: *(hopeful)*

Perhaps they'll change their mind and decide to share what they've found.

MATT: *(mutters)*

I wouldn't bet on it.

BOB: *(almost nervously)*

Well, no... but... So, do we have a plan or…?

MATT: *(enthusiastically)*

Oh yes. Yes! We have a plan!

BOB:

Thank goodness for that, at least! And what does that involve, may I ask?

MATT: *(excitedly)*

We're going out on the airwaves.

BOB: *(taken aback)*

We're doing WHAT!?!

MATT:

Hospital radio, Bob. My friend Tim has a show every Tuesday. Drive-time!

BOB:

Oh... I'm not sure about that, Matt... Tuesday is now... Today!

MATT: *(not really listening to Bob's concerns)*

Yes, yes, indeed. We''ll be leaving in about an hour, mate. We're going to broadcast to the nation. I know you don't like public speaking but it's okay, I'll do all the talking! I'm even looking forward to it!

BOB: *(surprised)*

Do that many people listen to hospital radio? Sick people, I guess.

MATT: *(trying not to be too preachy)*

No! No! You're behind the times, Bob – anyone can listen on the internet.

BOB: *(attempting to catch up)*

Oh! Okay... And people actually listen? *(Matt nods)* And then what? We

173

hope that someone out there might be able to help us with our little problem?

MATT: *(confidently)*

Yeah. Why not? Somebody who knows something is bound to be listening!

BOB: *(slightly teasing)*

Really? You sound surprisingly sure of that. More than I would be.

MATT: *(assuredly)*

That goes without saying, Bob. Born pessimist! I have a feeling, that's all!

BOB: *(attempting a winning smile)*

Well, I'm glad to hear it. So you speak and I'll just nod encouragingly! I must admit I have so many questions to ask about this myself.

MATT: *(taking charge)*

It's fine, Bob. You can ask them on the way there. Just come with me for support and I'll say all the big stuff. Okay? Right. Get that coffee drunk, get a slice of toast down your neck, get dressed and then we'll head out!

(Bob is about to speak – but Matt has already returned to the kitchen)

27. INT. THE RADIO STATION, EARLY AFTERNOON

(The scene begins at a radio station – but we do not yet recognise these characters. Firstly we meet Tim, who is the host of the show that Bob and Matt will be going on – then there is Pam, the show's Producer)

TIM: *(excitedly)*

I really can't wait for tonight's episode, Pam. It'll be a good one, I think.

PAM: *(bluntly)*

Don't you always say that every week, Timothy dear? I hope you mean it! It's just our ratings have been dropped quite dramatically of late and I can't help but think that your choice of guests has been partly responsible for this!

TIM: *(hurt)*

Pam! I'm shocked that you'd say that.

PAM: *(trying to reason with him)*

Oh come on. You've got to admit that we've been scraping the barrel a bit of late as far as guests are concerned.

TIM*: (still cross)*

Well, that's charming, isn't it? When did you last invite a guest on the show?

PAM: *(slightly ashamed)*

About five years ago. That chum of mine from the Teddy Bear Museum.

TIM: *(calmer)*

Oh yes. I remember him. Edmund something. I think I went to school with him. Didn't he come dressed as a teddy bear? Still – that was a pretty interesting conversation now you remind me. But FIVE YEARS AGO!

PAM: *(attempting to be helpful)*

At least I'm realistic enough to realise that nobody else that I know has anything interesting to say. You need to go on social media. Set up a Facebook page or something – get people to suggest interesting people that we can have on the show. Don't make that face, it could work!

TIM: *(prickling again)*

Maybe but if you know so much about it then maybe you could do it. And what's more, I do still have a day job to hold down, freelance or not.

PAM: *(breezily)*

I don't want to start an argument. I know you're busy. But aren't we all? I just think that you need to admit that the standard of guests on your show have been pretty poor of late.

TIM: *(suddenly remembering)*

What about Emily? She spoke about bell ringing. That was only last month!

PAM: *(trying not to sound too critical)*

She was trying to crowdfund our audience to pay for the repairs to her frayed bell ropes, if you recal. That's pretty much all she went on about.

TIM: *(disappointed/apologetic)*

Well, if we can help... I mean at least she showed up. It gave us a show. I did try to steer the questions into slightly different areas of interest but I'll admit that she did keep going back to money.

PAM: *(sad/attempting to reason with him)*

Nonsense. Accept it; we're behind the times. Have you seen the audience download figures lately? It's painful viewing.

TIM: *(dismissing her)*

Oh, I never pay any attention to stuff like that.

PAM:

That's more than clear to everyone. You really should, you know. How are we ever going to improve if you act like you don't care about the show?

TIM: *(more level now, but still hopeful)*

Perhaps you're right; I've never really thought about it. Anyway I don't know why you're so worried. I can vouch for the guys that are coming tonight. I've known them for decades; more or less.

PAM: *(sarcastically)*

You KNOW them? Whoopee-do. Big deal!

TIM: *(ignoring her)*

I went to college with them – night class – film studies. About 20 years ago.

PAM:

Oh, so is that what you'll be talking about? Old films or something?

TIM: *(awkwardly)*

I'm not really sure, to be honest. We haven't really discussed it.

PAM: *(frustratedly)*

You invited them as guests but you never discussed what you're going to talk about? You do know that we start the show in less than an hour.

TIM: *(beginning to ramble)*

Sure... Sure. Well, originally I had planned just to make tonight's show me reading some of my poems interspersed with a few song choices by listeners but then I got this email from Matt asking if I had a free guest slot for tonight. I emailed him a couple of months ago suggesting that he

177

come on maybe with Bob but I hadn't heard from him. He's always pretty busy.

PAM: *(coolly)*

How accommodating of you.

TIM: *(with wavering positivity)*

I guess Matt must have something good to say if he got in touch like this.

PAM:

"Something good..." Hmmm... We can but hope. It had better be exciting!

TIM: *(finally losing his temper)*

I don't know why you're being like this, Pam – is this some kind of passive aggressive way of telling me that someone somewhere involved in this station doesn't want me to be here anymore. YOU for instance.

PAM: *(remaining relatively calm)*

I never said that,Tim, dear... But believe me when I say that there are people out there who have an eye on your show – this radio station even.

People with ambition and quite probably more money than sense.

TIM: *(pushy)*

You know something. What's going on here!?

PAM: *(cutting him off)*

I don't want to discuss it. I should probably leave you to choose your records now.

TIM: *(calling after her – still annoyed)*

You do know that we went digital about five years ago, right?

(But Pam does not reply – she heads quietly for the door quietly)

TIM: *(sounding distressed)*

PAM... PAM!!! PAM!?! WHAT DO YOU KNOW?

(But there is no reply

SCENE 28. INT. RADIO STUDIO, LATE AFTERNOON

(Meanwhile, Bob and Matt are arriving. Matt is driving and parks in one of the designating parking spaces set aside for visitors to the station)

MATT: *(apologetically)*

I'm afraid we're a little early.

BOB: *(positive)*

Better late than never, I guess.

MATT:

I'm sorry. Attack of the nerves.

BOB: *(surprised)*

What are you nervous about exactly?

MATT: *(with nervous excitement)*

Oh... you know... It's the radio. It's a big deal. I don't want to come over sounding like I'm stupid.

BOB: *(slightly sarcastically)*

Are you sure this is a good idea, mate? I mean – if it makes you so nervous. It can't be good for the blood pressure.

MATT: *(not noticing the sarcasm and responding unaware)*

No, no. Not at all. I'll be just fine. I'll just sit here for a while and take a few deep breaths. After all you'll be there to encourage me.

BOB: *(distracted)*

I hope you don't expect me to say much. As I said before I'll nod and smile but that's about it.

MATT: *(taking his turn to be sarcastic!)*

Which always works so well on the radio, of course.

BOB: *(casually)*

Oh well, you know what I mean. I'll make all the right approving sounds and maybe grunt a bit, introduce myself if I really must. That sort of thing.

MATT:

You're a pal, Bob – how WOULD I do it without you?

BOB: *(distracted)*

I'm not sure you'd notice if I was there, or I wasn't to be honest. Uh oh. I can feel vibrations!

MATT: *(surprised)*

That's weird. So can I! It's my phone, I think. At least I hope it is.

BOB: *(in agreement)*

Hmm… That's odd. Mine too…

(They both take out their mobile phones – holding them out in front of them – staring at the lit screens. neither man answers their device)

MATT: *(curious)*

Who is it? Debs?

BOB: *(with a grin)*

Yes! How did you guess?

MATT: *(drily, with a chuckle)*

How did I guess that it's your wife calling you, Bob? Why! I'm clairvoyant! I'm not sure who's calling me. It's a library number.

BOB:

To be fair we're actually really busy right now. We probably ought to go into the station. After all, that's what an answer phone is for. Taking messages. Should we do that? Should we really do that?

MATT: *(cutting the phone ring off)*

We should… DONE!

BOB: *(nervously)*

Debs is going to kill me. Done! I'm switching it off.

MATT:

Just say you had no reception.

BOB:

If she needs me, she knows where I am. She'll probably ring the station in the middle of the show to ask what I want for dinner just to irritate me.

MATT:

We can only hope. *(he nods towards the station)* Shall we go in?

BOB: *(gingerly)*

Go on then. Let's.

(After a moment, the two of them head for the entrance. Pam is watching them from her office, Tim greets them at the door but somebody else is also watching from the car park – filming everything with a phone)

A WOMAN FOR ALL REASONS

EPISODE TEN: BAITED BREATH...

BY NICK GOODMAN

SCENE 29. LIBRARY – NEVILLE'S OFFICE. DAY

(Emily sits in Neville's office using his computer. She has a head set on and before her on the screen is an elaborate layer of applications including a POV video of Bob and Matt from a distance in the car park. Another is a list of people on an online chat room. The office door is ajar just a crack)

EMILY: *(into the headset)*

Well, at least we know where to find them. Well done, your Honour.

MARQUIS OF HAMILTON: *(Voice-Over)*

Do I go any nearer?

EMILY:

No, I know where they'll go. I have this show up on Neville's PC.

MARQUIS: *(V-O)*

Make sure you close it down before Neville gets back or we'll both be in the shit.

EMILY:

That vacuous nerd wouldn't know what's on his computer.

MARQUIS: *(V-O)*

Where are they going anyway?

EMILY:

A radio show. No prizes for guessing why! I happen to know the show. They've interviewed me in the past. I talked them about my bell-ropes, Pretty small-scale local radio usually but tonight – the world is listening!!

MARQUIS: *(V-O)*

Why don't we just tune in and learn the truth?

EMILY:

I will be tuning in, but you and I know it won't be the whole story. But it would be useful to know how far they have got.

MARQUIS: *(V-O)*

Why are they on there then?

EMILY:

They want info from other people. We must know what other people are getting from this.

MARQUIS: *(V-O)*

I'd rather not know! Can I go home?

EMILY:

How did you ever get the nerve to make porn? You're like a jittery child!

MARQUIS: *(V-O)*

So would you be if you'd become wedged in this business as long as I have!

EMILY:

Well, I have. The only difference is that I enjoy it.

(Clicking on Google)

I've located where Bob and the girl live.

MARQUIS: *(V-O)*

What of it?

EMILY:

They've all been home since last night. Unpacking. Downloading. The message, your Honour. The one the police failed to get out of that phone.

MARQUIS: *(V-O)*

Oh no!

EMILY:

Just this one thing. Then home. And a piece of the glory, I promise.

MARQUIS: *(V-O)*

That's breaking and entering. I can't afford to be seen doing that. One sniff that I'm involved in something illegal and it'll be all over the papers.

EMILY:

Oh, come on now, your Nobility – just wear a disguise or something!

(The door creaks open and Kirsten enters. Emily immediately collapses her screen and expands a list of books with tick boxes next to them)

Kirsten! Don't you ever knock?

(Kirsten has changed slightly. Her cocky, weary indifferent attitude is replaced with a worried, contrite demeanour)

KIRSTEN:

Sorry, the door was open. Where's Neville?

EMILY:

Regional meeting. He'll be back by five. I suggested that he just go straight home afterwards but he insisted on doing the late shift. What do you want?

KIRSTEN:

Err... I just came in to sign for my overtime.

EMILY:

Couldn't it wait until tomorrow when you're in next?

KIRSTEN:

Neville insisted that it needed to be done by today otherwise it's too late.

EMILY: *(grumpily)*

He would say that. A stickler for the rules our Neville. Hold on.

(With bad grace, Emily moves to the desk alongside the computer and searches through drawers with increasing frustration. Kirsten's eyes stare at the computer screen. A low rumble of a distant radio show is heard)

KIRSTEN:

Emily, I am sorry about last night. I was so tired. I realise there are things that I shouldn't get – in fact CAN'T get involved with.

EMILY: *(without looking up)*

Some are born to greatness – others have greatness thrust upon them. Others just say 'Err?' You'll learn. It's academic anyway. As far as I'm concerned, this whole Walsh business is an absolute con.

KIRSTEN: *(softly)*

Well, I certainly hope so. It would make things a lot easier.

(Emily slaps the overtime sheet down. Kirsten picks up a pen and instantly signs along the line)

EMILY:

I shan't be in tomorrow. The boiler is being disembowelled. I want you to concentrate on 'Foreign Travel', please. It's in an absolute shambles!

KIRSTEN:

Sure. Will do. I'll be off now, though.

EMILY:

Okay. See you Monday. And close the door. If Tatum needs help, she can call one of those muppets from Registration.

(Kirsten closes the door but, on the other side, she lingers, looking around. All is quiet. A girl is processing a customer's printing. The customer is busy on her phone. Kirsten puts an ear to the door as discreetly as she can)

EMILY: *(back on headset)*

Sorry I was interrupted…

MARQUIS: *(V-O)*

Who by?

EMILY:

Someone you really don't want to meet.

MARQUIS: *(V-O)*

Who's that?

EMILY:

Kirsten. Your former star.

MARQUIS: *(V-O)*

The stroppy kid...

EMILY:

You didn't hire her for her sweet temperament.

MARQUIS: *(V-O)*

Did she hear you?

EMILY:

You flatter yourself. You'd think she'd recognise your voice after all this time?

MARQUIS: *(V-O)*

Well...

EMILY:

Look, no more talk. I need to record that show. You need to get round to Deb and Bob's house. I'll text you the address.

MARQUIS: *(V-O)*

What am I doing there?

EMILY:

Get in there. The message which that old barmpot Alice recorded. It must have been downloaded at some point. If you can't find anything in writing, just nab the computer.

MARQUIS: *(V-O)*

On my own???

EMILY:

Think! Improvise! You are a film maker, for Heaven's sake!

MARQUIS: *(V-O)*

I am inspired by the naked form. Bums, boobs. Not burglary!

EMILY:

Then imagine this house is a model that you're undressing very slowly. Rip its clothes off and find what you're looking for. Get gone. Report back soon.

(Emily clicks off)

Toffs!! One-bloody-track mind.

(Emily closes the POV application and enlarges one with a radio icon. She also clicks up one with a digital sound recorder, adjusts the settings and begins recording what is being broadcast from the radio site)

Now, let's see what the boys know!

(By now Kirsten has glimpsed the scene through a crack in the door. She looks anxious. She instantly searches Emily's reception desk. She

looks through a book of addresses. She selects one of them and then writes it down on the back of her hand, once done she leaves quickly)

SCENE 30. RADIO STATION STUDIO. DAY.

(Bob and Matt sit in the Studio guest seats opposite Tim who is on air. Behind a glass panel. Overlooking proceedings, is Pam watching the scene with increasing aggravation)

TIM: *(in presenter mode)*

…And there will be some more travel news at three o'clock. But time now to meet my guests of the afternoon. Two gentlemen who are actually old friends of mine. We were at college together studying film making. That was twenty years ago, but this is now. They don't look a minute older. Will you please welcome Matt Spencer and Bob Tully.

(Canned applause)

Guys, it's so good to see you, how have you been keeping?

MATT:

Bit tired at the moment, Tim but then we've had an eventful couple of days.

TIM:

So, I heard. Some of which you can share with us this afternoon. Some, I understand, which you can't – for legal reasons.

MATT:

Well, to be perfectly honest we're not completely sure that you'll believe us – and we absolutely understand why that might be – it's a pretty strange tale that we have to tell. As far as the legal reasons are concerned, I guess we're just being cautious. There are a lot of names involved in our story. Some people might link up with others and it could get nasty!

190

BOB:

(Cagily, eyeing the glaring Pam in the control room)

Well, let's see how we go as the story unfolds.

TIM:

Now stories are something you lads had a passion for, even back in the day. You always had some writing on the go. I was convinced you were going to be a kind of double-headed JK Rowling.

MATT: *(slightly bashful)*

Aww well. It could still happen.

BOB:

To be completely honest with you, I've actually had writer's block for ages now. So, Matt – my loyal mate here – said let's go on a… well…

TIM:

A bear hunt?

BOB:

An anything hunt. Let's fall in love with writing again. Let's get stuck in.

MATT:

So, we went to the library. I had a tip off.

(Pam furiously grabs a phone, dials and is seen speaking soundlessly)

TIM:

Now as I remember, boys, you were both very keen on writing sci-fi stories – with the occasional murder thrown in for good measure.

Am I right?

BOB:

Yes. That's true. We love all that stuff. We so wanted to make it big.

MATT:

But what we're uncovering – slowly but surely – may top an alien invasion!

BOB:

So, it all started with the local library.

MATT:

Somewhere out there is a lady we need to find.

TIM:

Tell me about it!

(Behind the glass, Pam slams the phone down and contemplates the controls before her. She fiddles with them – avoiding eye contact with Tim)

BOB:

Everyone is looking for this woman. She is very influential with a fascinating background.

MATT:

She is tying the country in knots. It's gone viral.

(The lights go out and the power is cut. Behind the glass, Pam straightens with a look of satisfaction)

TIM:

I'm sorry about this. I'm not sure what's going on. Everything's suddenly gone kaput. It happens sometimes. It'll be up again in a minute, I'm sure.

MATT:

Rather suspicious if you ask me. Just as we were getting in our stride.

TIM:

Oh, come on, lads. Don't tell me you're all into conspiracy theories?

BOB:

Matt's right, though – it's not a conspiracy. Someone wants us to shush.

TIM:

The question is can I … oh, just wait a minute.

(Tim pulls out an extension lead and fiddles under the desk. He then takes the lead and plugs it into a control panel on the other side of the room. He laughs in triumph as the lights and power return)

(To Bob and Matt) I didn't tell you the other course I took when we were at the old place? Electrical engineering!

(Behind the glass, Pam looks in disbelief and then slumps, head in hands)

(Tim presses the red 'Live' button)

TIM: *(To microphone)*

Ladies and gentlemen, I can only apologise for the hiccup. We're back!

(To Bob and Matt) Boys, you were saying?

193

MATT:

Well… The lady I was trying to tell you about is called Constance Walsh; Lady Walsh, in fact. Local pillar of society. A long time ago too.

BOB:

What we don't know is what happened to her. For some reason, a lot of people want to stop us from finding out.

(Tim looks across his controls as a red incoming call light flashes)

TIM:

Well, you know I gave your story a great deal of thought. I felt it might be useful if we got some listener input. Out there, in the ether as it were.

(Bob and Matt exchange uneasy looks)

BOB:

Oooookay, what kind of input?

TIM:

We have someone on the line who tells me they can shed a little light on your mission. I think you're going to find this fascinating.

MATT:

Tim, you mean you told the listeners about our mission before the show???

TIM: *(Genuinely bemused)*

Well, yes. I gave them a bit of a hint.

MATT: *(To Bob)*

I bloody well knew this was a mistake!!

TIM: *(a mite uneasy how things are turning)*

Well, we have our caller on the line now. Hello caller, would you like to tell us a little about yourself.

(The voice is elderly, firm and female)

VOICE:

Good afternoon boys. I'm delighted to be speaking to you at last. Or at least having a two-way conversation. My name is Lady Walsh, but you can call me Constance.

(Both Bob and Matt look stunned)

SCENE 31. BOB AND DEB'S LOUNGE. DAY.

(The front door opens onto the lounge and in stagger Debs and Alice. Between them is a weary CB, dressed in a Groucho Marx rubber mask with handcuffs dangling from his wrist. All breathe a collective sigh)

DEBS: *(to CB)*

Well, you had us round to yours, the least we could do is return the compliment; we might all get a cup of tea this time too.

CB:

Does your visit count? Considering that you weren't invited.

ALICE:

We'll call it quits. You did arrange a cosy chat with the police for us.

CB:

Yes, sorry about that, Gran. That was Emily stirring things up. I was on 'Planet Zog'; a radio channel for her Walsh-ship.

DEBS: *(taking her coat off)*

At least we got the message. CB, do take that mask off. You're safe now.

CB: *(peeling mask off)*

I am?

ALICE:

Well, no one has penetrated our safe haven yet!

DEBS:

Auntie, that almost sounded obscene.

ALICE: *(to CB)*

Would you like that cup of tea, then dear? Debs? Yes?!

CB:

Just a glass of water for me, please.

(Alice leaves the room to fetch some water)

DEBS: *(to CB)*

So, what possessed you to handcuff yourself to a filing cabinet?

CB:

The council. They're in on it. Like the cops.

DEBS:

In on what?

CB: *(looking around nervously as he speaks)*

The Walsh gig. An acting pal of mine, Darcy told me that the plaque had dates.

DEBS:

Dates?

CB:

End dates! Lady Muck… She's dead! Darcy says so.

DEBS:

Did you see this?

CB:

No, the plaque has changed. A new plaque. One with no dates on. There is a mammoth cover up here. You must see that.

DEBS:

But…but we know she's alive!

(Alice enters the room with tea tray but freezes in her tracks)

ALICE:

DEBS! Auntie is telling you to keep Mum!

(Alice stares in alarm, beyond Debs, at the curtain)

CB:

Oh, come on – I'm on your side!

DEBS:

What's up Auntie?

ALICE:

Walls have ears. But more importantly, they ALSO have trainers!

(Alice points. Everyone follows her point. A pair of trainers are seen underneath the curtain. Everyone sees this and looks surprised. The curtain swishes back to reveal a tall figure with a Donald Trump rubber mask. He holds in one hand a small box – a dismantled hard-drive from a computer. Debs looks over at her machine and sure enough there is a ragged hole in the middle of it! In his other hand, the figure holds a hammer)

BURGLAR:

Nobody move – or the hard-drive gets it!

DEBS: *(pointing)*

Look what you've done to my PC!!

BURGLAR: *(insincerely)*

I'm really sorry – but I'm afraid it was necessary. *(Waving the box)* Now I need what's in this!

ALICE:

And what is that, exactly? What makes you think you've any bargaining power, hey? I think we outnumber you rather dramatically, don't you? Well? I asked you a question. You could do me the courtesy of a response!

BURGLAR: *(sneering)*

Oh, come on lady. Don't even pretend you're in control here. You know exactly what I want. The message. You must have downloaded it by now.

198

DEBS: *(cool, patronising and surprisingly calm)*

I'm sorry, buddy but you aren't making any sense.

(The room is at check-mate – with both factions now as bold as each other!)

BURGLAR:

It's a rush job, I know – but I really do need to know what the message said.

CB:

Well, at least he hasn't threatened us. Still, a please would have been nice.

BURGLAR:

Shut up Groucho. When I've finished with the hard-drive, I may still go for the soft option! Don't try me because I'm really not kidding.

CB: *(backing off with a whisper to his companions)*

He isn't from Walsh. She would not have condoned clobbering people.

ALICE: *(to Burglar – not even slightly scared)*

Aren't you a bit posh to be a burglar? Fallen on hard times, have we?

BURGLAR:

Let's just say it's complicated!

ALICE: *(reasonably)*

Let's just say that's life! Anyway I'm pretty sure that if we sit down over a cup of tea then we can come up with an arrangement that benefits us all.

BURGLAR:

I don't think so, lady. Let me pass. Someone wants this... really badly.

ALICE:

If it's the message you want then why not just ask? I have it written down.

DEBS:

Auntie!

ALICE:

Would you rather have your precious memory smashed to bits?

BURGLAR:

Written WHERE?

ALICE:

Why, it's here... *(Picking up a notebook)* Here we are.

(Alice gets nearer. The intruder raises a hammer.)

BURGLAR: *(beginning to panic)*

It's a trick! Put that down and let me pass.

(Alice rolls her eyes and lets the notebook flutter from her grasp. She looks at Debs with a withering expression)

ALICE:

I tried. Debs, you saw me try. You know what, I despair, I really do! *(To Burglar)* Now look, I'm losing my temper now! If you leave the drive here and say no more about it.

BURGLAR:

You half-demented woman! This is my ticket!

CB:

To what exactly?

BURGLAR:

You could not even begin to…

(The doorbell rings. The intruder jumps out of his skin. CB leaps up and wrestles the hard drive. The intruder raises his hammer, more to ward him away rather than hurt him but Debs has his hammer arm. CB wrenches the hard drive free. Debs and Alice pull the burglar down on his knees)

ALICE:

Now Scooby Doo, eat your heart out! The time has come to reveal our assailant… Shall we finally see who this presidential upstart is?

(The mask is pulled off revealing a dishevelled Marquis of Hamilton, looking exceedingly embarrassed)

And who the hell are you?

(There is now an urgent knocking on the door)

DEBS*: (nodding to CB)*

Better get the door.

(CB opens the door to a desperate-looking Kirsten)

KIRSTEN:

I was too late! I'm sorry I overheard Emily sending him over here. Did you beat him to a pulp, already? I wouldn't blame you.

ALICE:

And who might 'him' be?

KIRSTEN:

'His Honour' the Marquis of Hamilton. Film maker and wheeler dealer.

MARQUIS:

Who is this little brat?

KIRSTEN: *(walking closer)*

Sorry your Grace, last time we met I had all my clothes off!

ALICE:

Marquis! It is indeed a pleasure... of sorts...

DEBS:

So that explains the disguise.

(Kirsten walks right up to him)

KRISTEN:

It was 'Bored Belinda' wasn't it? Straight to download. I was sixteen and needed the money for... well, that's none of your business, to be honest...

MARQUIS:

Well, come to that, I needed the money too. You went in eyes wide open.

KIRSTEN:

I had to – there was more than me to think about. I was pregnant if you must know. Something that men like you never give a second thought to.

DEBS: *(to Marquis)*

I would say you've been caught with your trousers down but you might enjoy that! Either way we have you by 'em!! Breaking and entering, aye?

MARQUIS:

Emily holds the cards. She can ruin me and maybe that's what I deserve.

ALICE:

Maybe. But we also hold the cards. Help us or we'll ruin you first!

MARQUIS:

You don't understand, she can flip an embargo on a certain YouTube video just... *(snapping fingers)* like that! She knows how to pull police strings too!

DEBS: *(by now completely lost)*

What is going on?

MARQUIS:

All I know is that it is some kind of treasure hunt. But altogether stranger. This lady is turning the country upside down.

DEBS:

But it's all covert. All online based. Why has it stayed that way?

KIRSTEN:

Speaking of which, your blokes have gone on the radio to talk about all this.

CB: *(quietly furious)*

The idiots! That is going to cause chaos.

ALICE: *(sarcastically)*

Not at all like handcuffing yourself to the council filing cabinet.

CB:

No one saw. Come to that, no one cared!

ALICE:

Debs, can we tune in on this radio show, so you think? Will they still be on?

MARQUIS:

It's no good, it will all be over by now.

ALICE:

Shut up your sleaziness and make yourself useful.

(Alice takes a screwdriver from a drawer and hands it to the Marquis)

You can jolly well put that hard drive back in Deb's computer, you little vandal! Don't say you can't – because you'll stay here until it's done.

DEBS: *(fiddling with her phone)*

I can get it on my phone. What's show is it, Kirst?

KIRSTEN:

It's the local hospital Drive Time show. I think the guy's name is Tim?

CB:

I know Tim. I used to radio ham with him.

KIRSTEN: *(sounding vague, distracted)*

Is that so?

(CB takes Deb's phone)

CB:

Here – I'll find it.

ALICE:

I'll switch on the blue rinse speaker.

DEBS:

Tooth!

ALICE:

Tooth?

MARQUIS:

Blue tooth.

ALICE: *(to Marquis)*

Speaks the expert. Trust you to know something blue!

(Debs leaves CB to fiddle with the phone and switches on a speaker on a bookcase. At first there is a distant warble but then the show comes

205

across clearly on the speakers. An elderly voice halts them all)

VOICE:

Ah at last. You worked it out, eh Alice? You always were a game bird. So… we're all here. My two intrepid boys. My two intrepid girls. That scarecrow from the rail hut. The naughty public schoolboy. At last, I have your complete attention! Now maybe I can get a word in edge-ways…

A WOMAN FOR ALL REASONS

END-GAME:

YOUR WHOLE LIFE STRETCHING OUT BEHIND YOU...

BY NICK GOODMAN

SCENE 32. INT. TENTBURY HALL. NIGHT

(A large country home called Tentbury. A grand hall with pillars, ending in a huge desk with screens above it. Debs, Alice, Bob, Matt, CB, The Marquis and Kirsten wander curiously, yet nervously into the room. An elderly man dressed in the clothing of a royal butler steps out to welcome them all. He has long white hair, slightly covering his eyes)

BUTLER:

Welcome! You all received your text messages, I take it?

(All in the party nod or grunt, clearly still bemused)

Now as you know Lady Walsh has made herself known to you. But she wishes to meet all seven of you in-er – person. In a completely non-sinister and productive way, you simply know too much!

MATT: *(gulping)*

Does that mean we won't be leaving?

BUTLER:

It may be that you may not want to leave after she has spoken to you.

ALICE:

Spoken to us? So, she is actually here?

KIRSTEN:

She must be well wrinkly by now.

DEBS: *(softly)*

...and deaf.

ALICE: *(turning to Deb)*

...and what?

DEBS: (Louder)

AND DEAF!!!

BUTLER: *(paying no note to the background chatter)*

Come this way, please...

(The butler leads them to the end of the hall. Large portraits hang on the wall. Five of them at the very end are of Constance Walsh. A large screen shows chat feed. Another small screen shows shares and transactions. A CCTV camera glares down at them from a wall)

MARQUIS: *(nervously)*

Are we being recorded?

BUTLER: *(slightly smug)*

How do you like the boot on the other foot?

(The butler goes behind the giant desk)

KIRSTEN: *(curiously musing)*

Foot..... *(Looking curiously at the Marquis)* Foot.

MARQUIS:

Daddy should have disinherited me when he had the chance! Too
sentimental, that was his trouble. Oh well. Either way I'm done for.

DEBS:

WE might all be. Apparently "We know too much!" Too much what
though?

BOB:

Who knows, love. It's a pity we can't enjoy the fact though, isn't it?

(Kirsten answers a text message on her phone. She reads it)

KIRSTEN:

Sorry, its Emily. "Have you seen Neville?" Derr no, I've finished work.
I don't hang out with the dweeb.

BUTLER: *(clearing his throat)*

Can I have your full attention?

KIRSTEN: *(texting as she speaks)*

Sorry! You have my full attention.

BUTLER: *(continuing after a brief pause to command attention)*

You have all worked hard and been in touch in many and various ways
with Lady Constance Walsh. It may be far after her time, but you will
all be familiar with Charlie and The Chocolate Factory? Willy Wonka?
As I'm sure you will recall, he summoned those children and groomed
them to take over his chocolate empire...

CB: *(enthusiastically)*

I always liked Mike Teevee best. He was going places.

209

DEBS:

I don't like the word groomed. It's a bit too creepy for my liking.

MATT:

Let's face it – so was Willy Wonka.

BOB:

So, Lady Walsh wants us to be a little old lady in her place?

BUTLER: *(Becoming slightly flustered)*

No, no! But her influence has been felt in the world. Things have got out of hand, and she needs your help in the 'Willy Wonka' way.

BOB:

Are you saying she never intended to send out Golden Tickets as such, but now she wants us to help her?

BUTLER:

She can't manage anymore. She has become an online viral phenomenon as you can see from feeds on the screen above me. She is leaking out all over the place! Err... Well, you know what I mean! Her assets are in danger.

MARQUIS:

Isn't it time she spoke to us herself? I'm sure you need a rest, Granddad.

(The butler steps away from his desk, takes Alice's arm gently and leads her to a large elaborate door to the right-hand corner of the room)

BUTLER:

Alice isn't it? You remember her I understand.

ALICE: *(charmed)*

That's right. She taught me the piano and how to ride a horse. Not at the same time of course. Not to say Morse Code. I could play the chop sticks in Morse Code by the time I was ten. Be ready for anything she would say.

(Smiling, the butler opens the door which leads through to an old study. It is a cosy, war-time-era haven for a tomboy. Grey haired, glasses on the end of her nose, Lady Walsh is sat is a wing chair threading a needle, apparently busy undertaking some stitching work on part of a Union Jack flag. She is also waxen and completely motionless. The others follow bar CB)

BUTLER: *(with sadness)*

She has been working on that since 1953.

(CB enters behind the others, holding a blue plaque that he has just retrieved from the surprisingly cluttered butler's desk)

CB:

This is the original plaque from the theatre isn't it? She died in 1953, whilst preparing for Coronation Day. *(Reading the plaque)* At the age of 88.

BUTLER: *(sadly)*

She's served her Royal Highness. Without rest.

(Alice grabs the butler by the lapels and shakes him)

ALICE:

You had her stuffed, you insensitive monster!

(The shaken butler's wig dislodges. A suspicious Kirsten moves forward and whips the wig off. Underneath is Neville, looking sad and ashamed)

KIRSTEN:

Neville!! I thought I recognise your voice from the way you said "foot"!
What the hell are you doing? You were supposed to be doing the
banking!

ALICE:

You know him??

KIRSTEN:

Know him? He's my boss at the library!!

MATT:

I would never have guessed. I remember him arriving!

(Neville snatches his wig back and folds it away preciously)

NEVILLE:

For the record I didn't stuff her. I wasn't even born at the time. It was
Cooper D'Cartre, the Anglo-French taxidermists.

(Neville moves closer towards the immobile Walsh, almost in awe)

Her family at the time interpreted her dying wishes rather literally. She
wanted her memory to live on. So along with all the business and
information, they had her stuffed. Very patriotically I think you'll agree.
Every scrap of information of her life was recorded and stored. Every
interview that was ever conducted. She became a thriving, ongoing,
living figurehead of patronage and local business. But there was a
clause in it all. We couldn't tell a soul that she was dead. That was what
her family laid down and tied up in red tape so tight you wouldn't
believe.

CB: *(holding up the plaque)*

I'm not sure I understand their reasoning. And also... what about this?

NEVILLE:

We didn't know it was there. Someone in the arts discovered she had died but didn't know it was a secret. We had it removed for continuity purposes.

CB: *(annoyed)*

...And closed The Rook Theatre to boot. A bit drastic.

NEVILLE:

No, that really was the local council. But it was a happy coincidence.

BOB: *(Clicking his fingers at Neville)*

Your office! Now!!

(Neville ambles out of the study to his desk beyond. The others follow, mesmerized by Lady Walsh's petrified form as they go)

NEVILLE:

Cooper D'Cartre are now the lead taxidermists for France's best loved pets. That was once they had run out of hoity toities wanting heads on the wall.

MATT:

(To Neville) Number one question – who are you?

KIRSTEN: *(frustratedly)*

I told you who he is!

DEBS:

Alright then, why is he?

NEVILLE:

Constance Walsh was my Great, Great… *(Pause)* I think that's all the 'Greats' – Aunt. I took over from my father running the businesses. She was patron of practically everything as I'm sure you've already gathered.

CB: *(baffled)*

But she's dead! Sorry to point this out, Squire. Who spooked me then? Who came through 'Crystal' and nobbled me?

ALICE: *(curious)*

What did I pick up on my phone?

KIRSTEN: *(confused)*

…And what are you doing in the library?

BOB:

You've wasted our time, mate! All this has been a wild goose chase! I'd also like to echo what CB said - why all this mystery about Lady Constance?

MATT:

Don't expect any simple answers, Bob. This one's a bloody fraud!

NEVILLE:

Stop there everyone! There are answers I need too, you know!

DEBS:

Not so many though!

(Neville sits at his desk, clicking some buttons on his computer keyboard. He leans back to survey his accusers as if considering what to say next)

NEVILLE:

It was never meant to be like this. The enormous – and interactive I might add – acquisition of personal and business data was encoded. None of Constance Walsh's supposed ongoing presence was within this.

DEBS:

Presence? What, as a ghost?

NEVILLE: *(Fidgety)*

Well, no – maybe – but I'm coming to that. Things have leaked out from that supposed encoded top-secret part of what we call the Walsh Web. Somehow someone cracked the code. When you two *(Pointing at Matt and Bob)* came onto the scene I assumed it was you two.

ALICE: *(indignantly)*

And don't forget Debs and me! We're the brains behind the boys!

NEVILLE:

That I do believe – well, you were my Plan B suspects.

DEBS:

Charming! Ever-under-appreciated!

KIRSTEN:

So why come to the library?

NEVILLE:

An independent income. I have all I want here except for self-respect.

(Bob and Matt each mime violin playing – it is clearly a bit of an in-joke between them as they chuckle when they see the other one doing so)

I also needed to learn as much IT as possible to work this...

(Neville gives his hi-tech desk a resentful thump. Up comes Edmund (as featured in Episode Seven) on the screen above him. Edmund is sat in his bedroom, surrounded by soft, brightly coloured cushions, he is live online.)

Ahh there you are. Sorry to disturb you.

(Turning to the others) My media monitor – my man in Sydney!

(To Edmund) Any clues as yet, Eddie?

EDMUND:

No, but the chat room followed the radio show.

BOB:

I knew we shouldn't have done it!

EDMUND: *(to Bob)*

I'm glad you did. It took the whole situation to the wire. That's why we had to pull you out. It was the only way we could find out for sure whether you were friend or foe. The only problem is seventy-five thousand followers are thumping their phones, tablets and laptops wanting more.

NEVILLE: *(to Edmund)*

Well, its Team Walsh on the case. Catch you later.

(Neville cuts the connection and turns back to the assembly before him)

That was Edmund. My damage limitation. He's been hyping and fantasying the facts just to throw people off the scent. He has the time to monitor events. He's very rich, you know – a very generous ally to have on your side.

KIRSTEN: *(looking hopeful)*

Is he single?

NEVILLE:

He also lives with his mother.

KIRSTEN: *(under her breath)*

Oh! Well, that makes two of us! That's more common ground, I'd say…

CB:

So, to get back to the leak, do you have any fail-safe?

NEVILLE:

What do you mean?

CB:

I got mind zapped by something,

ALICE:

…And we were chased by imaginary dogs.

NEVILLE:

The Walsh Web contains a virtual reconstruction of Constance Walsh for training purposes. I think they call it artificial intelligence these days. This is as near to that as we can get.

MARQUIS:

Giving the impression that she is still alive.

NEVILLE:

Legally we had no choice. It was bound in legislation.

MARQUIS: *(now as frustrated as CB and Bob)*

Bound in legislation, why? Why did they insist on it? How stupid!

NEVILLE:

You think so? Take away her date of birth – and death, of course – and you have a figurehead. So, you don't know who caused the leak?

MATT:

Frankly, we thought it was someone playing a game. A treasure hunt.

NEVILLE:

No… No… No! It's quite the reverse. This treasure needs to be put back in the box and locked up tightly.

(Pause) How did and you and your friend get in on the Walsh world?

(Bob and Matt look at each other puzzled and then turn back to Neville)

BOB:

Well Emily, of course. She recruited us through Matt.

NEVILLE: *(taken aback)*

She did what?

MARQUIS:

…And me before them! And Billy before me *(Pause)* Poor Billy!

BOB:

She wanted to know whether Lady Constance was still alive.

MATT:

And more importantly, why?

NEVILLE:

What was she playing at? I didn't know she had a hand in any of this.

BOB: *(with a smirk at the memory)*

She gave us a slide show and presentation of all that she had discovered. She even had leaflets – which I presume came out of the library budget.

(Once again, Neville thumps the much-abused hi-tech desk)

NEVILLE:

Damn cheek! Right under my nose!

KIRSTEN: *(To Neville)*

You run the whole gig and Emily wasn't on your radar?

CB:

I half expected her to be here. She stitched me up before.

ALICE:

I think she was interested in the ghost bit. The missing link, so to speak. That's why she sent... *(Pointing at the Marquis)* …the last of the red-hot lovers there to do us over.

219

(Neville slumps down, worried – deep in thought)

BOB: *(to Neville)*

It seems she's limbo-ed under your radar.

(He points to the screens above…)

Are you sure you don't know where the leak has come from?

NEVILLE: *(incredulous)*

Emily? She's just a control freak librarian.

ALICE:

Oh, Neville!

NEVILLE: *(waggling a finger at the screens)*

But I have gone through this network thousands of times. I haven't slept.

KIRSTEN:

Meanwhile Emily seems to have taken over your office. She's using your computer, you know. All sorts of online stuff – that's how I overheard about His Grace doing over Matt and Debs' place.

NEVILLE: *(clutching his head)*

Wait a minute – you – she – MY office!

KIRSTEN:

When I picked up my wages. I saw her.

(Neville looks increasingly horrified)

NEVILLE:

Oh no! No... No... No...

(Neville flips through a diary on his desk and runs his finger down a column of writing. He spots something. He collapses back in his chair with a groan)

DEBS:

What is it?

NEVILLE:

11th February. I activated a link for a client. I activated it using the library computer!!

MATT:

Search history would have done the rest.

KIRSTEN:

You pillock!

CB:

Why then did she need all of us if she had the info already leaking?

(Alice touches the back of CB's neck and makes him jump)

ALICE: *(to CB, whispering)*

The ghost!

NEVILLE:

That I can't explain. Like I say there is an interactive profile of my Great, Great... whatever – Aunt in the web, but no way could it act randomly.

CB:

Or take people over.

MARQUIS:

She takes people over all right. She –

(The Marquis looks dumbstruck. All look at him suddenly wondering what it is that has caused him to break off mid-sentence)

DEBS:

What?

MARQUIS: *(ashen faced)*

She still has a tag on me!!

(The Marquis whips out his mobile and fiddles with it)

With all this, I forgot. It's still on!

KIRSTEN:

That's all we need. You're a pillock too!

MARQUIS: *(panicky)*

Switch it off! Someone switch it off!

NEVILLE:

Too late for that. She's been monitoring us, she's up to speed. She knows we're onto her. We must stop her. Let's go, no time to lose!

(Neville leaps from his desk and heads for the door but Matt bars his way)

MATT:

Hang on, what exactly is in all this for us?

NEVILLE:

What?

MATT:

You've had us chasing our tail. We were recruited by Emily. Why shouldn't we help her instead of you?

BOB:

Especially as all this was because you made a bloody fool of yourself.

NEVILLE:

But you will be serving your country to help protect the dignity of one of its finest stalwarts.

(Bob and Matt pause to think)

BOB:

That will do for now. Come on!

SCENE 33. INT. REFERENCE LIBRARY. NIGHT.

(Emily still has an open channel on Neville's office PC. She has heard everything! The Marquis' panicked voice comes over the speakers as he fumbles to break the link as they head for the library. Eventually he succeeds)

(The library is in partial darkness. It is after hours and no-one but Emily is left. She is rushing around the aisles of the library, books in hand, in a state of both frustration and elation. Down one aisle she drags a chair to the centre of the ref library, where a table is set with a

candle standing ready. She dumps the books onto the table and attends to a device that she has set up in front of the table. It is a microphone stand lashed up with wires, topped with an old-fashioned radio loudspeaker. She then checks the library clock: nearly 10pm. Like a mad scientist she flips through the books, bookmarking passages, and muttering to herself. She stops to think then produces the pamphlet she created about Lady Walsh (as seen in Episode Three.)

EMILY:

In case I forget anything important.

(She gets herself comfortable and presses a switch on her microphone stand. She then closes her eyes. A gentle static starts up. A few moments concentration and then she slowly begins to mutter, her voice rising up)

Constance Walsh. Dame. Entrepreneur. Patron. I call to thee. I say I call to thee. I'm not sure why you would accept 'thee' rather than 'you' as a term of address, but you have to play the game, I guess. I have discovered some details about your life. I have followed your career. My name is Emily Bradnock. My Great Great Grandfather was the only man you ever loved – as I understand. Peregrine Pope was his name. I think you'll remember him? You nearly married him. Your brother talked you out of it. So, Constance – you could say that I am your spiritual Great Great Grandchild.

(A few aisles away, as quiet as possible, Bob, Matt, Debs, Alice, CB, Kirsten, and the Marquis creep closer to the bizarre séance, listening intently)

I know you came to CB through his old rubbish radio set. I give you my own rubbish radio set up. I perceived that you would prefer to communicate through this kind of technology from your own era. You reached out to CB. You are there! You cannot hide from me any longer!

(Neville stares through a gap in the books in disbelief)

Many have reached out to you since you have leaked back into the world; a whole gang of them in fact. A nest of vipers. Family too. Speak only to me Constance. For the love of Peregrine, I am the only one that you can trust.

(At last there comes a faint voice…)

VOICE:

Is that you Emily?

EMILY: *(suddenly bolt upright)*

Grandmama, I'm here!

VOICE:

What do you want of me?

EMILY:

To talk. We must talk. You must let me in. Confide in me. I am that Grandchild you never had.

VOICE:

Idiot girl… You are nothing of the kind.

(Alice appears at the corner of the nearest aisle in Emily's view. Hers was the voice all along)

ALICE: *(mocking)*

You're just a very naughty girl!

EMILY:

Get away from here you silly old cow. This is a seance!

ALICE:

You want her soul because you think it's out there.

CB:

Sheer sentimental crap. It's an AI-developed aspect of the Walsh Web.

ALICE: *(to CB)*

Oh, do be quiet!

NEVILLE: *(stepping forward)*

If she is out there, she must be left alone. Haven't you done enough damage? You cracked the code.

EMILY:

Of all the devious, sanctimonious two faced… it was you that ordered all those books about Walsh?

NEVILLE:

I wanted her represented in the book stock.

EMILY:

Very careless! Your actions alerted me. I began putting it all together.

NEVILLE:

But why?

EMILY:

My family never forgot the name Walsh. I could have been where you are!

NEVILLE:

I am blood kin to her. I run the Walsh Web. I am your superior. In that capacity, I order you to stop this invasion.

EMILY:

And disappoint my public. The storm I've created won't just go away.
Millions will know all there is to know - all I want them to know,
should I say! But I will be including my Great Great Grandfather in the
equation too. That's where I came in. It's my calling and I'm committed
to it.

KIRSTEN:

Emily, you can't do this.

EMILY: *(to Kirsten)*

Rank has its privileges. *(To the others)* Since all your efforts to locate
her on a spiritual plane have failed, I have had to jerry rig my own link
up.

NEVILLE:

You released the web, but you haven't been able to control it and collate
the information. Lady Constance's 'presence' is the key to it all!

KIRSTEN: *(angered)*

You put my family in jeopardy will all this public crap!!

EMILY: *(scathing)*

What family? A dead mother? A scrounging drunken father...

KIRSTEN: *(screaming)*

My little boy, you bitch!!

*(Kirsten lunges for Emily but moves too close to the loudspeaker.
Something strange happens... Kirsten stares ahead and goes rigid. Matt
and Bob run forward to help her, but Alice holds them back)*

ALICE:

No, don't touch her. I think Lady Constance has landed!

DEBS:

Should I phone for an ambulance!?!

ALICE: *(reassuringly)*

No, I think she'll be alright…

EMILY: *(outraged)*

Child! What have you done?

BOB: *(to Emily)*

What have you done, you mean!?!

(An ethereal smile and a sudden calm descend over Kirsten, and she begins to speak with the speech patterns and vocabulary of a much older woman)

KIRSTEN:

All this shouting! Calm down everyone. Calm down.

NEVILLE:

Sorry Auntie – Great, Great Auntie.

KIRSTEN:

Where am I?

EMILY:

The local library. Did you hear what I said earlier?

KIRSTEN:

Did you ask me something?

EMILY:

Do you know WHO I am?

KIRSTEN:

Not exactly.

NEVILLE: *(getting nearer)*

Auntie, my name's Neville. I'm your Great, Great Nephew. Possibly even greater. I run your business and family affairs.

EMILY: *(to Kirsten)*

He betrayed you! He opened the floodgate to your business and personal secrets. I can help you. I WANT to help you.

KIRSTEN:

Do you dear? Well, that's very good of you.

EMILY:

Peregrine Pope. You remember him, don't you? He proposed to you.

KIRSTEN: *(frowning)*

Peregrine? I... I...

(Kirsten turns in thought. In the shadows, the others confer)

BOB: *(to Matt)*

What's going on?

MATT:

The séance seems to have worked. Old Lady Connie has taken over
Kirsten – just as she did CB. Only with very different results of course.

CB:

I was hypnotised. There was nothing supernatural about it.

ALICE:

Don't be so stupid. Your old junk-box couldn't hypnotise anyone.
Neither could her set up for that matter. Your mind just couldn't
rationalise it. Which is why she came to you in bits and pieces at the
shack.

CB: *(almost in a whisper)*

Well, what are we supposed to do?

MATT:

Nothing. We have to hope Neville has history on his side.

BOB:

History?

DEBS:

You heard Emily. She's the sprog of some old lover.

MATT:

Suitor if you don't mind! They didn't have lovers back then.

ALICE:

Oh yeah? Well, that's news to me.

(Back at the table)

EMILY: *(pointing at Neville)*

He's a careless incompetent. He let your information out for all to see!

NEVILLE:

It wasn't like that, Auntie. The modern world has computers. So much information is instantly available, but I protected all the personal stuff...

KIRSTEN:

Peregrine! I remember him!

EMILY: *(excited)*

You do? Do you remember him proposing?

KIRSTEN: *(smiling distantly)*

I do so. He loved me... I... I...

EMILY:

You loved him too! Why didn't you just say yes to him? One short word!

KIRSTEN:

But I couldn't possibly...

EMILY:

Well, why ever not?

KIRSTEN:

It wouldn't have been right. I was already engaged to four others.

CB: *(hollering)*

Gold digger!!

EMILY: *(horrified)*

Wha.....?

KIRSTEN:

I lost all idea of what I said to whom. Best to leave it, I thought. I had so many meetings to attend. Dogs to look after. Scout camps to run.

EMILY: *(crying)*

But you loved him! You did, didn't you?

(Kirsten comes up to Emily and puts her hand on her shoulders)

KIRSTEN:

Sweetheart, I loved everyone. That's why I helped all those services. I did my bit... for my country. My chance to make a difference. It was a thrill. Besides, what would you have done with my world?

(Pointing at Neville)

Just look at my Great Great .. err ... Nephew? Juggling two jobs. Overworked. Lonely. Confused. Desperate for help.

NEVILLE: *(to Kirsten)*

So, you do know me!

(Kirsten clasps Emily's head in both her hands)

KIRSTEN:

Now it's time you to do your bit. Whatever gobbledegook you unlocked, lock it up again. I'll help you.

(Both girls walk trance-like into Neville's open office and sit by the PC)

NEVILLE: *(calling out)*

Great Great Auntie? You do know you'll go home as soon as the link is cut.

KIRSTEN: *(from the office)*

If you say so dear. Goodbye.

(Overcome Neville slumps into the now empty séance chair, sobbing with relief. The others move across to him)

ALICE: *(looking on)*

Poor Constance. A true legend.

BOB:

A reluctant legend.

ALICE:

She never did get around to marriage – for better or for worse.

MATT:

What's happening?

CB:

Hypnotism. I bet she wanted to find out the secret.

BOB:

Pity she's not awake to appreciate it.

DEBS:

Are they resetting the privacy settings? That code thingy?

MATT:

That and hopefully blockers on all unwelcome callers.

NEVILLE:

I'm confused. If I don't know the new password, how will I get on the system back at Tentbury?

CB:

Well, you wanted help, didn't you?

NEVILLE:

What?

ALICE:

Yes, that's true. *(To Neville)* You made out you were a Willy Wonka figure when you summoned us to your hideout. But you're really more the Wizard of Oz. A little man struggling to control a big machine. I think it's time you showed us your Willy again!

(Everyone looks shocked)

…Of the Wonka variety that is!

NEVILLE:

Well, we can talk about that when we are back at the hall.

DEBS:

Well, I could do with a pint after all this.

NEVILLE: *(looking at his watch)*

It must be gone last orders by now.

CB:

We know a gaff which never closes. Well, it never seems to...

(There is the sound of a crash. All look towards Neville's office. Emily lies slumped over the computer. Kirsten reels dazed. She comes gingerly out of the office. She pops some gum in her mouth and chews it, it seems to give her a certain confidence, even reassurance.)

DEBS: *(hugging Kirsten)*

Kirsten, you little darling. You saved us all!!

KIRSTEN:

I did?

CB:

Devilishly clever impression! *(Alice jabs CB in the ribs)* Oww!

BOB: *(To Kirsten)*

It's over. Neville has a proposition for us all.

KIRSTEN: *(vaguely)*

A proposition? Why does that ring a bell?

(The Marquis crawls from the shadows, stopping at Kirsten's feet)

MARQUIS: *(in a whimper)*

Your Ladyship, from your view up on high, please forgive me! I beg forgiveness for my indiscretions. I will serve you to my dying day.

(Kirsten leans down to face him and blows a bubble gum bubble which pops in his face. She then giggles and kisses him)

KIRSTEN:

You know what? You are strangely sexy when you grovel. You still up for serving me, like you promised to?

SCENE 34. INT. 'THE LUMINARY TAVERN'. NIGHT.

(All back to the actor's pub for the finale – our story ending in a pub, as it began. All except Emily are in 'The Casket' as seen in Episode Six. Everyone, including Alice, are downing a pint)

BOB: *(Checking his phone)*

Well, the hoax warning is out. But there will always be those you won't believe it was a hoax. But that's social media for you. The conspiracy theories will be fun to read.

CB:

They were certainly fun to create.

MATT: *(raising a glass)*

To Kirsten – and Constance Walsh. A team amongst teams!

(All raise a glass to Kirsten, who blushes)

KIRSTEN:

I just don't remember any of it.

CB: *(sarcastic)*

Yeah right!

MARQUIS:

Well, you might have told me when you were out of the fluence!

KIRSTEN:

No way, I was enjoying it too much!

ALICE: *(to Marquis)*

You still owe me a hard drive. Your Grace. How about grovelling to me – or maybe you can buy me a completely new computer with your fortune?

(The Marquis looks a little unsure as to how to react – but Alice clearly isn't joking. Everyone else turns to Neville who is looking into his pint)

NEVILLE: *(wistfully)*

"I'm a good man but a bad wizard…"

MATT:

What possessed you to hire Emily in the first place?

NEVILLE:

Her I.T. skills were superb. She was also suitably odd. I thought it would detract from me and my activities. I also needed to learn from someone good to keep up with all the high-tech data at Tentbury.

DEBS:

Instead of which she learnt from you!

NEVILLE:

If I hadn't made that transaction from my office! Still, I won't do that again!

CB:

What are you going to do with Emily?

NEVILLE:

Well, when she woke up…

BOB:

Don't tell me! All memory of recent events was wiped from her mind. It was all like a bad dream. Not that old cliché!

NEVILLE:

No, not quite. She was noticeably quiet, but she offered her resignation fairly promptly before going home.

ALICE:

Where is she going?

NEVILLE:

To live with her sister and her family in Bangor.

ALICE:

Does her sister know this?

NEVILLE: *(Smiling)*

I doubt it. But it'll make for a nice surprise.

CB:

It will, indeed… Now Mr 'Bad Wizard'…

NEVILLE:

I owe you all a great deal for saving my Great Great – possibly even greater – Aunt – from public exposure. But it's nice to know she is still amongst us one way or another. Gone but not forgotten.

CB:

Albeit in the form of a mannequin.

(All frown at CB who relents...)

Sorry.

NEVILLE:

Kirsten, would you like to be become my Deputy Head Librarian?

KIRSTEN: *(putting a playful hand on the Marquis' knee)*

I have had a word with his Grace. We have decided to go into partnership. You wouldn't think it to look at him but he's actually quite excited about it!

MARQUIS: *(allowing himself a smile)*

It's my way of giving something back to society.

ALICE: *(raising her eyebrows)*

Now that *is* a cliché.

DEBS:

You're giving porn back to society???

MARQUIS:

Oh no! Socially aware films.

KIRSTEN:

About single mothers for a start!

NEVILLE:

You're going to need patrons.

MARQUIS:

It would help.

NEVILLE: *(to Marquis)*

The Walsh Trust has enough of those. Keep the sleaze out we're all yours. *(To Kirsten)* On condition we can have you part time at the library.

(Kirsten laughs and happily swigs her pint)

KIRSTEN:

It's all coming together!

MARQUIS:

I'm still worried. Emily told me she had one of my naughty films on X-Tube and could break the embargo on it.

KIRSTEN:

You believed her? Look mate, if you can't see it, how do you know it's even there? Although it sounds like it'd be in good company on that site, anyway!

MARQUIS:

You don't sound too worried. So, do you mean....

KIRSTEN:

She was pulling your whatsit. And for once you didn't want it pulled!

(To CB) We'll need an engineer. Would you be up for that?

CB:

Oh, I can't keep up with all this modern stuff.

MATT:

Only because people didn't teach you. They just elbowed you out. You'll be okay.

DEBS:

It will get you out of that crappy railway shed too.

CB:

It will take some time to getting used to it.

NEVILLE:

The technology?

CB:

No, being wanted again.

KIRSTEN:

Bob, Matt, we're going to need script writers.

MARQUIS:

I've got scripts!

KIRSTEN:

Like I say, we're going to need ACTUAL script writers!!

MATT: *(to Bob)*

Told you I would get you writing again!

BOB:

How will we ever top this little escapade?

We've had… SEX! *(Pointing at the Marquis)* VIOLENCE! *(Pointing at CB who rubs her head)* GHOSTS AND GHOULIES! *(Pointing at Kirsten)* …and a big button pushing BADDY! *(Pointing at Neville)*

NEVILLE: *(affronted)*

I'm not a baddy!

BOB:

Only joking! Although we'll never really know whether Lady Constance was here in spirit or some virtual intelligence. Like Alexa gone mad!!

KIRSTEN:

What we would have in mind for scripts is something a little more down to Earth, perhaps – less alien invasions and a little more heart.

DEBS:

An admirable intention – something like 'Cathy Come Home'?

MATT:

In the past it would've been 'Cathy Come Home – to Mars'! Actually, I'm still convinced we could do something really big with that idea, one day!

NEVILLE:

Well, that may be… But if you could write us some promotional pieces for the Walsh Trust then that would be the icing on the cake.

(To Debs) and Debs…

DEBS:

Oh no, I don't want any fancy jobs thank you, I'll miss my soaps too much.

NEVILLE:

Well, okay then. I think that about wraps it up.

ALICE: *(putting her glass down firmly)*

Hold it, what about me?

NEVILLE:

No disrespect meant. But what ABOUT you Alice?

ALICE:

Well, I do think that perhaps I deserve a little piece of the cake – whatever that may be… you know… considering…

NEVILLE:

Considering WHAT, Alice? Just tell me…

ALICE:

Well, you forget – I actually met Constance Walsh? Not only that but if it wasn't for me then things would have taken five times as long to work out… Who was it got Debs on the case? Who came looking for these two twits? *(Pointing at Matt and Bob)* Who recorded a vital clue? Need I go on?

243

MATT:

Don't you want to take it easy after all this, Alice?

ALICE:

No, I bloody well don't!! You haven't given my contribution a moment's thought, have you? Well thank you so very much!!

(Alice storms off. Debs makes to hurry after her, but Bob waves her back)

BOB:

Maybe best to give her a minute…

MATT:

She's completely right, of course. We've not given Alice her dues.

NEVILLE:

Hmm… You're right, of course. Let's start again, shall we?

DEBS:

Absolutely. I think that would be only fair and sensible…

(Meanwhile, Alice storms down the stairs to the bar below where Graham the barman has his head on the bar, where he appears to be crying)

ALICE:

Hello dear, what's up?

GRAHAM:

It's gone! The head!

ALICE:

What's head?

GRAHAM: *(looking up, tear-stained)*

Sweetheart, there is only one head. Johnny. The one that was up there covered in blood. Hated the wretched thing myself but the punters adore him. What's Big Bruno going to say? They'll take it out of my wages – although goodness knows how you'd put a price on poor old Johnny…

ALICE: *(leaning on the bar)*

Pull yourself together man! What are you talking about?

GRAHAM: *(tightly)*

There is a paper gauche severed head that lives on the shelf up there. It was left over from the previous ghouls that ran this boozer. We call him Johnny. Someone has stolen it. Savvy, Grandma?

ALICE: *(releasing Graham)*

There, that was nice and clear. There have been enough muddy waters, lately.

GRAHAM:

You're with those two writer blokes, aren't you? Can't they investigate this?

(Alice makes to return to 'The Casket' then stops, turning back to Graham)

ALICE:

No! Nuts to them. I'm the one you need to solve this for you.

GRAHAM: *(dabbing his eyes)*

You? You can you do that?

ALICE:

Yes... It's becoming a habit! I was the brains behind our investigation. I'm not even kidding. Pour me a gin and tonic and I'll make some notes.

(Smugly Alice dusts off a bar stool, removes a small note pad and pen from her handbag and takes a seat as Graham prepares her drink)

Right! Now tell me that whole story from the start...

THE END

FACT FILE

EPISODE ONE

The idea for this first episode came about around May 2016 and the first draft was finally typed on Saturday 2nd July 2016. As there were two main characters, I asked Nick what he would like "his" character to be called – he chose Bob and I chose Matt. I initially christened Bob's wife – Debs but told Nick at that time that he was welcome to change that if he had another idea but he was happy with Debs. I also gave Matt the surname of Spencer in this first part. It was written all in one sitting on the morning of Saturday 2nd July. I returned to episode 1 between the 4th and 8th July 2020 for 'final' editing and rewrites and also added one or two new lines – and also lost one or two but I was happy with my changes. (PC)

EPISODE TWO

Scenes 4-6 were written between 16-19 July 2016. This was the first piece of original creative writing that I'd worked on since the summer 2011 when a supernatural thriller book I was working on with a friend fell through. In keeping with the library reference in episode ,1 I decided on a library setting. I actually wrote the episode in Salisbury's Reference library which has been my favourite place to retreat to and write for nearly 20 years. Emily Bradnock was named after my first Infants School teacher, Tessa Bradnock. She too was quite an entertaining performer although the resemblance ends there. I felt Debs was holding something back in the first episode, so I twisted that still further. The claustrophobic cliff-hanger was loosely based on a sinister childhood memory of being shut in a garage over the road from our house, whilst a group of freaky older kids experimented with clothing dye. In real life, Miss Walsh was an old lady with unfortunate stockings who visited a writer's group and told us to research local history and odd events at our library. This was the same meeting where I first met Paul. As this project is very close to home in its parallels with our lives, I thought that it would be good to make her the focus of the mystery. I enjoyed the experience of writing episode 2 and looked forward to further instalments. (NG)

I began working on final formatting etc of this episode around the 9th July 2020. (PC)

EPISODE THREE

Having read the second episode during the week beginning 25th July 2016, I wasn't immediately sure where to turn for episode three – which was my second episode for the project. I was aware that I didn't want to spoil any ideas that Nick might be thinking up leading off from his cliff-hanger and so I left the script for a few days, returning to it whilst away in Kent on Thursday 4th August 2016. It was whilst having a long bath that morning that I decided that what I really wanted to explore next was what Debs might have been up to. I began working on the plot between the 4th and 5th of August and started the actual writing on Sunday the 7th August – writing Scene 7 in one sitting that morning. Scene 8 took a little longer as I was back to work, but I wrote it during lunchbreaks between Monday 8th and Wednesday 17th August 2016. The final scene, number 9, I wrote on Friday the 19th August 2016, the majority of it at work during my break. The ending of the episode was originally going to go on beyond the point where Alice saw the body, but I decided that it was better to end things at the point that I did and leave a question mark over what has been unearthed...

Originally Auntie Alice was going to appear on the phone in Scene 7 and then appear again in Scene 9 – but she came across so strongly when I was writing Scene 7 that I couldn't see Scene 8 without her and thought it worked better to have her threatening the librarian during that scene. I also made notes for Scene 8 where Auntie Alice pretty much threatened Emily to get the information that they needed – as good as grabbing her by the scruff of the neck and pushing her up against the wall. In the end this didn't seem to fit into the scene or with Auntie Alice's more urbane personality. (PC)

EPISODE FOUR

There had been a bit of delay between Episodes 3 and 4. This was partly due to other project commitments, work and visiting a very old school friend. My work on Episode 4 finally began on the 21st September 2016. I decided that what we needed was a bit of a run-around episode. This was a similar way of thinking to Lee Freeman when he worked on the other Paul-initiated project 'Aulde, Gray and Wrinkly' back in 1992: a section of the story where the characters let off steam and get some action. This seemed the right time to do something similar now that the characters were established. But, at the same time, I didn't want to lose any story development. With the arrival of Kirsten in Episode 3, I saw the possibilities of a Lucy/Peppermint Patty type relationship between her and Emily (for those of you familiar with 'Peanuts' and Charlie Brown) and things getting too tempting for Emily to keep in the shadows anymore. Alice was a good ally for Debs, who the lads increasingly resent for her interference. I finished the rough draft on the 5th October 2016, whilst on holiday in Kent (where Paul had been when working on Episode 3!). I enjoyed it very much and felt it flowed out me a lot easier than Episode 2. Finally, the phone call where we learn Bob is a delivery driver was added on the type-up on 7th October. This was to address the question as to what he did for a living and was also a parody of a similar conversation a mutual friend of ours had many years ago when rung by his boss in the middle of organising a Dr Who convention! (NG)

Note: On the blog where I was storing the early drafts of these episodes, we had it noted down in the "cast" list that Bob was an Assistant Theatre Manager. I have no idea where this idea came from as it is never actually referred to in the scripts. I amended this list when I noted that Nick had decided on an alternative career for Bob. (PC)

EPISODE FIVE

I had Nick's script for Episode 4 for a couple of weeks before I got a chance to read it – which I eventually had time to do on Tuesday 25th October 2016. My ideas for episode 5 came quite quickly – scene by scene. Nick had allowed himself 4 scenes rather than 3 in episode 4 (it's okay, it's allowed – there are no rules!), but I decided to return to a 3-scene episode. The next problem – having worked out my scenes and a rough plot-line – was when to actually write my episode to fit around other distractions. I had hoped to get a bit of time when I was away in Venice for my birthday between the 6th and the 11th of November 2016 – but that time just flew, and I didn't get a chance to write anything. In the end I didn't get to flesh out these ideas until after the New Year when I actually finished the first scene and completed the final two scenes in just a matter of days during breaks at work in mid to late

February, giving it one final look-over on Friday 24th February 2017. I was really interested to see where the story went next... (PC)

EPISODE SIX

I neglected to record when I started writing this chapter but approximately late March/early April 2017. I had not intended to step outside the three scenes per chapter last time and only realised when Paul mentioned it in his notes last chapter. I redressed it here though slightly cheated, treating all scenes in 'the Tavern' as one scene. The main purpose of this episode was to logically follow through the events of Paul's episode and also expand on CB and it also takes us on another turn with a twist at the end. 'The Tavern' was based partly (and certainly physically) on 'The Haunch of Venison' in Salisbury where the Salisbury Operatic Society was founded, and many actors are known to hang out. The pub's previous gruesome theme was inspired by the 'Haunch's history of haunting and its displayed mummified hand. The Morse message is still free to be scrabbled and lead to other things and CB has a lead of his own. I also thought it was high time we discovered what did happen to the Marquis of Hamilton. Ill health over Easter 2017 and other commitments left me drained and unable to complete the chapter for a while, finally finishing up on Bank Holiday 1st May 2017. (NG)

EPISODE SEVEN

I received Nick's episode six on Monday 1st May 2017, but due to other creative projects and various holidays I didn't get a chance to start writing episode 7 until late June, early July 2017. I actually came up with the idea for my episode on Monday 17th July 2017 and did a scene break-down. This episode removes us slightly from the main events of the previous episode but I wanted to develop a broader sense that some of the things that are happening are somehow being shared with a wider network of interested parties. Scene 20 was eventually written in one sitting on Thursday 31st August 2017, with scene 21 written in a similar standalone writing block on the 14th September. Scene 22 was written between the 18th and the 19th September 2017. Following this I did some reworking of the three scenes between the 20th and 28th

September 2017, before sending the episode off to Nick to read. Overall, I hope that I am taking the story into some kind of new area which will also compliment what we have already written. There are definitely more questions than answers at the moment, but I hope it intrigues. What with the first two scenes being rather removed from the other events so far, I wanted the final scene to take us back into the story – now aware that at least some of the events are being watched by curious internet-users/subscribers in other locations. I also enjoyed the discussion in Scene 21 about the difference between drama and reality TV, partly inspired by the sorts of conversations my father has when he claims to hate soap operas but then watches a western with all the same elements as a soap – just with added cowboys and Indians. He also listens to 'The Archers'. Dad, that's a soap! *shakes head sadly* I also enjoyed writing the beginnings of the seduction – especially when a strong female character is taking the lead and reversing stereotypical roles. Lucky Georgio! (PC)

The Twiddler mentioned in this scene was a reference to a villainous character I had created in 1977 for my home-grown sci-fi adventure series 'The Magnet Editor'. Further reading on Twiddler can be found in 'Magnet Memories – the Story of a Secret Series: 1977 – 1987' available from Lulu.com and Amazon. (NG)

EPISODE EIGHT

Work on episode eight was heavily delayed by work on a long-term book project that was coming to an end. I began planning the episode in early February 2018 on a week off from work. The legacy of Episode Seven is the revelation that our protagonists are being watched. I was keen to develop this, with a different example of it in every scene. Scene 25 cheats a little in being set both just outside and just inside the nursery. Were it a stage, the scenery could easily have been presented both as the actual area being in close proximity.

With Emily and Kirsten's story having come to a stop in Episode Six, I was keen to take them in a new direction so they could still contribute to the story. I thought it was time we met The Marquis who once becomes Emily's tool. His backstory is slightly based on a local public figure from times past! Also, I thought it would be nice to see a vulnerable side to Kirsten as she fears for her own privacy as 'Big Brother' – or rather online – is watching them. Miss Jameson is named after the actress Louise Jameson whose first TV role was as a schoolteacher in 'Cider With Rosie' on BBC 1.

Heavy snow and a couple more days off ensured that I wrote the last two scenes at home, finishing the handwritten draft on Monday 5th March 2018. I enjoyed it very much and looked forward to the next instalment! (NG)

EPISODE NINE

It took me a while to get down to writing this episode after I'd received episode eight – partly because I was busy with my podcast and partly because about four different books that I had been working on for 2-3 years all came close to being completed around the same time during the summer of 2018. In the end I finished the third scene on Tuesday 21st August 2018 before sending it on to Nick. I decided that I'd like to set the episode at a radio station because around this time I was reading my poems on our local Radio Wey every other month. The character of Pam was named after Pam Goodman, Nick's mum because she sadly passed away during the time that I was writing this episode and I wanted to somehow mark that in the script. The end of the episode reminds me a little of the end of episode 1 of Dr Who's 'Greatest Show In The Galaxy' – in which the Doctor and his companion, Ace, are about to enter the Psychic Circus – unsure what lies ahead of them. Here Matt and Bob aren't quite sure what lies in store within the radio station. (PC)

EPISODE TEN

Writing on this chapter was very delayed due to a rush of final work on a book that I was writing, and Paul contributed to (submitting his piece in 2014) called 'Life After…Magnet Memories – The Return of the Secret Series 1988-1994'. With the manuscript submitted in mid-November, I was then free to work on chapter ten, completing the first draft on 14th December 2018. This far into the story, I re-read the last four chapters to ensure continuity points were maintained. I was keen to utilise the radio interview to bring things to a head and for Emily's pursuit in using the erstwhile disgraced Marquis in a slightly more dramatic way, despite the humour. The Groucho Marx disguise originated from a conversation that I had with my sister in the summer (as desperate light relief after arranging our mum's funeral) critically dissecting The Teddy Bear's picnic and pondering what disguise the narrator suggests people take to spy on the picnic! I was also keen to develop the plot points we have learnt so far. In addition to Paul's more recent experience with radio, I was a hospital radio DJ myself in 1997 and, like Tim, was faced with some internal resistance to the show that I presented. (NG)

When editing the final text, I noted that Nick had incorrectly given Matt the surname of Lincoln – quite understandably after all the time that we'd been working on the project – having forgotten that he'd been christened Matt Spencer in an early episode. I mention this only out of interest and not to shame Mr G. He became Matt Spencer again in the version of the story which you will most probably have read by now.

At the time of writing episode 10 – I was due to write an episode 11 – but we were beginning to feel that it was probably time to begin to wrap up the story although this might originally have been around episode 12. Sadly, I was struggling to reconnect with the story as the gaps between episodes became longer and longer and also my podcast is an ongoing project which doesn't allow for many other creative pursuits. Ironically – considering that the project was conceived because Nick had a writer's block – it ended with me having a mini writer's block where I couldn't see where to take the story next, and it also felt like Nick did know where it was going although apparently that wasn't the case until he began working on episode 11. (PC)

END-GAME:

It had been exactly a year since Chapter Ten. Around that time, Paul and I were feeling that the story was coming to a natural end and the next couple of chapters should wrap it up. I engineered a cliff-hanger for Chapter Ten that would deliberately bring the story to a head. The only problem is it was a cliff-hanger neither of us knew how to resolve.

During 2019, Paul and I had various discussions as to how to approach the last chapter. I suggested if I submitted a draft, Paul could develop it, making it a joint last episode. Our last joint written venture, ('Sutton Park - Prison in the Sun', 1993), was written on a bench in some public gardens. It would not have been practical to have repeated this.

One of the problems we were faced was that we have a scenario that could either have been explained away by science or fantasy. Going completely one way or the other could have disappointed. My solution was a mixture with a single question still hanging in the air. As it was still untitled, I offered a working title of 'A Woman for All Reasons'.

My draft Chapter Eleven began writing (in long hand) on Saturday 14th December 2019. I was resolved to use an established character as the force behind events. The unveiling of Neville was a gentle nod to 'Scooby Doo'. His elusiveness led me to believe that he would be a good reveal. I returned Edmund from Episode Seven. I felt there were hints there that suggested he was a little more than just an interested member of the public and had powerful connections. The only question left was – was Constance Walsh's ghost available online? Or did the website have a side effect? I also wanted the characters to return to 'The Luminary Tavern' for everyone to assess the situation at the end. This way we finished as we began with a talk in a pub. Paul had suggested Bob and Matt getting a call that might lead to another mission. I have here offered a slight variation on this with Aunt Alice going solo on her own mission!

Stopping only to listen to 'The Festival of Nine Lessons and Carols' on the radio, I completed my long hand first draft on Christmas Eve 2019 at 5.15pm. I spent the Christmas break typing up the draft and re-reading the previous chapters. I had approached the episode by getting down the solution in writing as I saw it before tweaking things after re-reading the previous scripts. The other way around I considered might have put me off with too many challenges.

I think the end result is a fun caper which never quite got as far-fetched as both Paul and I are capable of going. (NG)

Paul's concluding Comment:

As Nick had mentioned, there was talk of my adding some lines or even a scene to the final episode – but having read it through as I formatted it, I didn't really think that it required anything further as I thought that Nick had done an excellent job at wrapping up the story. Of course, as I've been working on the final project these last couple of months, I have added sneaky lines here and there along the way – and lost one or two – where it seemed appropriate, and I also did so during this final episode.

When working on re-writing and formatting the final book during the summer of 2020, I re-numbered episode 11 as 'End-Game' as my OCD was going crazy that we had an odd number of episodes. I did apologise to Nick at the time, but I think it looks quite good in the contents page to have ten episodes and then 'End-Game'. I'm a strange person, I admit it. I also have problems with sentences dropping one word onto a new line and will write extra words just to fill the space or edit the sentence back to just one line. Yup, always been like that. Doing it now with this very paragraph.

I finished working on the formatting and rewrites on the 21st August 2020, having forgotten to note the exact episode dates as I worked. Never mind!

Thank you for reading. We hope you enjoyed the story. Whether or not we ever get there, Nick and I have discussed a sequel, although it's funny to note that Bob and Matt had originally been intended as our 'heroes', but Alice and Debs ended being a far more effective team as the story progressed! (PC)

THE AUTHORS

Nick Goodman was born in Salisbury in 1968 and studied Drama and Theatre Arts and Radio Journalism at college. He has written several books and published scripts with Lulu.com. His guides and novels about his two home-grown series *The Magnet Editor* and *Life After...* have been published by Hidden Tiger via Amazon.com. He wrote and produced eighteen amateur video films between 1993 and 2008 and has had four of his plays performed on the Salisbury Stage. He has worked many times with Paul Chandler on projects in their long friendship.

He lives with his wife Alison in Salisbury, where he is an avid Anglo-Catholic, party lover and occasional actor! He has been writing since 1975.

Paul Chandler was born in Bournemouth in 1973 and has enjoyed a prolific creative career. Writing for his own home-grown series in his teens such as *Travellers, The Muddled Memoirs of Sir Roland Quaverall* and *Spectrum,* Paul ran the video spoof opera *Sutton Park* for nine years chalking up over 3,000 episodes. He has written scripts such as *A Cross to Bear* and the murder mystery *Touchwood* and numerous books for Lulu.com such as the *Mouse of Commons* series For many years he has written, published and performed poetry and currently runs his own Pod-cast site, *The Shy Life Podcasts.*

He has worked with Nick Goodman on a number of projects including the film *Sutton Park - Prison in the Sun* as well as acting in many Goodman-scripted productions.

Lightning Source UK Ltd.
Milton Keynes UK
UKHW020818121222
413794UK00016B/1141